Horatio Bridge

Personal Recollections of Nathaniel Hawthorne

Horatio Bridge

Personal Recollections of Nathaniel Hawthorne

ISBN/EAN: 9783337280956

Printed in Europe, USA, Canada, Australia, Japan

Cover: Foto ©Andreas Hilbeck / pixelio.de

More available books at **www.hansebooks.com**

PERSONAL RECOLLECTIONS

OF

NATHANIEL HAWTHORNE

BY

HORATIO BRIDGE

PAYMASTER-GENERAL U. S. NAVY (RETIRED)

What then? shall we sit idly down and say
The night hath come, it is no longer day?
The night hath not yet come; we are not quite
Cut off from labor by the failing light
Something remains for us to do or dare
Even the oldest tree some fruit may bear

" Morituri Salutamus"

ILLUSTRATED

NEW YORK

HARPER & BROTHERS PUBLISHERS

1893

TO

CHARLOTTE MARSHALL BRIDGE

THE WIFE WHO, BY HER WISE COUNSELS AND CHEERFUL AID, HAS
CONTRIBUTED LARGELY TO WHATEVER OF SUCCESS HAS
COME TO ME SINCE OUR MARRIAGE; WHO HAS BRAVELY
BORNE HER FULL SHARE OF LIFE'S BURDENS, AND WHO
FOR MANY YEARS, ENJOYED HAWTHORNE'S
FRIENDSHIP AND CONFIDENCE

THIS VOLUME

Is Gratefully Inscribed by

THE AUTHOR

PREFACE

———

THREE papers of " Personal Recollections of Nathaniel Hawthorne," recently published in *Harper's Magazine*, were favorably received, and have brought many letters, from strangers as well as from friends, urging me to publish still more upon the same subject.

I may therefore hope that a somewhat more extended account—in book-form—of Hawthorne will also be well received.

Accordingly, while taking the papers just mentioned as the basis of a volume, I have added some new material — including several letters from Hawthorne and General Pierce—now first published.

For many years I have resisted the persuasions of friends and publishers to write something of Hawthorne's life and character; to which end many recollections and not a little material, 'ill in my possession, might, perchance, be profitably applied. But, conscious of having neither the literary ability nor the critical skill essential to a biographical sketch of the great romance-writer or to an analysis of his writings, I shall refrain from attempting either, and here limit my narrative chiefly to matters connected with his college days, and to some incidents in his later career which, I think, have not yet been fully recounted by others.

The rules of chronology will not be strictly adhered to in the following pages, whatever may be the effect on the story. My main object is to give some facts—new and old—with little regard to structure or embellishment.

A somewhat busy life on my part and frequent separations, by sea and land, often broke the continuity of our personal association, but never that of our friendship. As an offset to those separations, however, I probably received more letters from Hawthorne, of a purely friendly character, than did any other man.

The earlier of those letters were all destroyed at his request. Some of the others—the publishing of which I trust no friend of his would disapprove—are herein given.   H. B.

"THE MOORINGS," ATHENS, Pa., 1892.

CONTENTS

CHAPTER I.

CHAPTER II.

CHAPTER III.

CHAPTER IV.

CHAPTER V.

CHAPTER XII.

CHAPTER XIII.

CHAPTER XIV.

CHAPTER XV.

CHAPTER XVI.

S.

S

31

ILLUSTRATIONS

PERSONAL RECOLLECTIONS

OF

NATHANIEL HAWTHORNE

CHAPTER I.

THE boyhood of Nathaniel Hawthorne has been chronicled by his son Julian, in the biography of "Nathaniel Hawthorne and His Wife"; by his son-in-law Lathrop, in the "Study of Hawthorne"; and recently, in an article in the *Wide-Awake*, by his relative Elizabeth Manning.

I shall therefore refer to that period only because Hawthorne's isolation and environment in boyhood seem to me to have had an important influence upon his character and conduct, even after he had come to manhood. He is described by his eldest sister (see "Biography," Vol. I., p. 99) as a "beautiful and bright boy; indulged not only by his mother, but by all his uncles and aunts."

Perhaps he might have been spoiled by this

I

indulgence, had not an accident brought on a tedious lameness which—though temporarily disabling—doubtless proved a "blessing in disguise" by keeping him aloof from the active sports of boyhood, and compelling him to seek occupation and pleasure mainly in books.

This enforced physical inaction, together with the seclusion of his mother's house and his long absences from Salem, combined to make him almost a stranger in his native town until he had left college; and these conditions must necessarily have had great influence in forming his peculiar character and shaping his later course.

With these preliminary remarks I turn to the subject of his college life, the delineation of which was the original and principal motive for the present writing.

A boy on going to college seventy years ago went under conditions so different from those of to-day that, to appreciate the situation, one must revert to the old stage-coach as, in the early morning, it passed from house to house, the driver blowing his horn to summon the passengers, and the family coming out to give their farewells and such cautions as would overwhelm with mortification a young fellow of the present day. In such a case, if a pretty sister made one of the family group, it would add materially to the interest felt in the new-comer. There may be as much susceptibility in the collegian of the present time, but we had a rather more *naïve* way of showing it.

The stage-coach gave better opportunities for travellers to become acquainted with each other than are afforded by the modern railway-car. Some old men will recollect the mail-stage formerly plying between Boston and Brunswick (Maine), drawn by four strong, spirited horses, and bowling along at the average speed of ten miles an hour. The exhilarating pace, the smooth roads, and the juxtaposition of the insiders tended, in a high degree, to the promotion of enjoyment and good-fellowship, which might ripen into lasting friendship.

Among the passengers in one of these coaches in the summer of 1821 were Franklin Pierce, Jonathan Cilley, Alfred Mason, and Nathaniel Hawthorne—the last-named from Salem, the others from New Hampshire. Pierce had already spent his freshman year at Bowdoin College, which institution his companions were on their way to enter.

This chance association was the beginning of a life-long friendship between Pierce, Cilley, and Hawthorne; and it led to Mason and Hawthorne becoming chums. There was no great congeniality between the two room-mates, owing partly to their joining rival societies, but more to the dissimilarity in their tastes and habits. Both, however, were well-bred and amiable, and they lived together harmoniously for two years.

A slight acquaintance with Mason led me to call at their rooms, and there I first met Hawthorne. He interested me greatly at once, and a friendship then began which, for the forty-three years of his subsequent life, was never for a moment chilled by indifference nor clouded by doubt. Though our paths in life, like our characters, were widely different, our friendship never wavered till the sad end came.

———

Hawthorne was a slender lad, having a massive head, with dark, brilliant, and most expressive eyes, heavy eyebrows, and a profusion of dark hair. For his appearance at that time the inquirer must rely wholly upon the testimony of friends; for, I think, no portrait of him as a lad is extant. On one occasion, in our senior year, the class wished to have their profiles cut in silhouette by a wandering artist of the scissors, and interchanged by all the thirty-eight. Hawthorne disapproved the proposed plan, and steadily refused to go into the Class Golgotha, as he styled the dismal collection. I joined him in this freak, and so our places were left vacant. I now regret the whim, since even a moderately correct outline of his features as a youth would, at this day, be interesting.

Hawthorne's figure was somewhat singular, owing to his carrying his head a little on one side; but his walk was square and firm, and his manner self-respecting and reserved. A fashionable boy of the present day might have seen something to amuse him in the new student's appearance; but had he indicated this he would have rued it, for Hawthorne's clear appreciation of the social proprieties and his great physical courage would have made it as unsafe to treat him with discourtesy then as at any later time.

Though quiet and most amiable, he had great pluck and determination. I remember that in one of our convivial meetings we had the laugh upon him for some cause, an occurrence so rare that the bantering was carried too far. After bearing it awhile, Hawthorne singled out the one among us who had the reputation of being the best pugilist, and in a few words quietly told him that he would not permit the rallying to go farther. His bearing was so resolute, and there was so much of danger in his eye, that no one afterwards alluded to the offensive subject in his presence. This characteristic was notably displayed several years later, when a lady incited him to quarrel with one of his best friends on account of a groundless pique of hers. He went to Washington for the purpose of challenging the gentleman, and it was only after ample explanations had been made, showing that his friend had behaved with entire honor, that Pierce and Cilley, who were his advisers, could persuade him to be satisfied without a fight. The lady had appealed to him to redress her fancied wrongs, and he was too chivalrous to decline the service.

Hawthorne, with rare strength of character, had yet a gentleness and an unselfishness which endeared him greatly to his friends. He was a gentleman in the best sense of the word, and he was always manly, cool, self-poised, and brave. He was neither morose nor sentimental; and, though taciturn, was invariably cheerful with his chosen friends; and there was much more of fun and frolic in his disposition than his published writings indicate.

CHAPTER II

HAWTHORNE dedicated but two of his books to friends—"Our Old Home" to ex-President Pierce, in 1863; and "The Snow Image" to myself, in 1850.

In the preface to the last he gives some pleasant glimpses of his college life, which present a better picture of his lighter occupations than can be found elsewhere; and it may be interesting to the admirers of his writings to have some of the statements in the following extract from that preface amplified and explained by one who was familiar with the scenes and incidents to which he refers.

In that dedication he says:

"Be all that as it may, there can be no question of the propriety of my inscribing this volume of earlier and later stories to you, and pausing here a few moments to speak of them as friend speaks to friend; still being cautious, however, that the public and the critics shall overhear nothing which we care about concealing. On you, if on no other person, I am entitled to rely

to sustain the position of my dedicatee.   If anybody is responsible for my being at this day an
author, it is yourself.   I know not whence your
faith came, but while we were lads together at a
country college, gathering blueberries in study
hours under those tall, academic pines, or watch-
ing the great logs as they tumbled along the current of the Androscoggin, or shooting pigeons or
gray squirrels in the woods, or bat-fowling in the
summer twilight, or catching trout in that shadowy little stream which, I suppose, is still wandering riverward through the forest, though you and
I will never cast a line in it again; two idle lads,
in short (as we need not fear to acknowledge
now), doing a hundred things that the Faculty
never heard of, or else it would have been the
worse for us—still, it was your prognostic of your
friend's destiny that he was to be a writer of fiction.   And a fiction-monger he became in due
season.   But was there ever such a weary delay
in obtaining the slightest recognition from the
public as in my case?   I sat down by the wayside of life, like a man under enchantment, and a
shrubbery sprang up around me, and the bushes
grew to be saplings, and the saplings became
trees, until no exit appeared possible through the
entangling depths of my obscurity.   And there,
perhaps, I should be sitting at this moment, with
the moss on the imprisoning tree-trunks, and the

yellow leaves of more than a score of autumns piled above me, if it had not been for you. For it was through your interposition—and that, moreover, unknown to himself—that your early friend was brought before the public somewhat more prominently than theretofore in the first volume of 'Twice-Told Tales.' Not a publisher in America, I presume, would have thought well enough of my forgotten or never-noticed stories to risk the expense of print and paper; nor do I say this with any purpose of casting odium on the respectable fraternity of booksellers for their blindness to my wonderful merit. To confess the truth, I doubted of the public recognition quite as much as they could do. So much the more generous was your confidence; and knowing, as I do, that it was founded on old friendship rather than cold criticism, I value it only the more for that.

"So now, when I turn back upon my path, lighted by a transitory gleam of public favor, to pick up a few articles which were left out of my former collections, I take pleasure in making them the memorial of our very long and unbroken connection."

———

Formerly the college grounds and the land adjoining included a great area of pine forest, with blueberry bushes and other shrubs for its undergrowth, and with foot-paths running deviously for miles under the shady trees, where, in their season, squirrels and wild pigeons might be found in sufficient numbers to afford good sport. The woodland gave a charmingly secluded retreat, and imparted a classic aspect to the otherwise tame scenery of the Brunswick Plains. Unhappily, in later years a public road was made between the campus and the quiet old graveyard, and a street was opened on another side, so that the grove has been sadly circumscribed. I am sorry to add that many of those "tall academic pines" have been cut down, leaving only their stumps to tell of their former existence and their destruction. The beauty of these woods made such an impression upon Longfellow's poetical mind that—fifty years later—in addressing the few remaining members of our class, he thus apostrophized the woods he so well remembered:

> " Ye groves of pine,
> That once were mine, but are no longer mine."

———

In our day one could wander for miles through this forest without meeting a person (except a stray student or two) or hearing a sound other than the occasional chatter of a squirrel, the song of a bird, or the sighing of the wind through the branches overhead.

By crossing the road leading to Bath, a town nine miles away, one came into another division of the pine woods, where the sandy soil was not so level, and through which ran the " shadowy little stream " that, after traversing the main street of the village and skirting the small elevation near Professor Cleveland's house, made its way to the river, a mile or so below the falls of the Androscoggin.

In this brook we often fished for the small trout that were to be found there ; but the main charm of those outings was in the indolent loitering along the low banks of the little stream, listening to its murmur or to the whispering of the overhanging pines.

There was one favorite spot in a little ravine, where a copious spring of clear cold water gushed out from the sandy bank and joined the larger stream. This was the Paradise Spring, which deserves much more than its present celebrity for the absolute purity of its waters. Of late years the brook has been better known as a favorite haunt of the great romance writer, and it is now often called the Hawthorne Brook.

———

Another locality, above the bridge, afforded

an occasional stroll through the fields and by
the river.   There, in spring, we used to linger for
hours to watch the giant pine-logs (for there were
giants in those days) from the far-off forests, float-
ing by hundreds in the stream until they came to
the falls; then, balancing for a moment on the
brink, they plunged into the foamy pool below.
Those who have seen such huge tree-trunks, each
possessing a certain individuality, approach in
groups or singly, and disappear, will understand
why it was so fascinating to "watch the great
logs as they tumbled along the current."

———

The Androscoggin River, one of the largest in
New England, bounds the village on the north,
while on the opposite side, and two or three miles
distant, lies Maquoit Bay (an inlet of the beautiful Casco Bay), which afforded a genuine marine
view, vulgarized though it was by the dilapidated
wharf and the two or three melancholy sloops that
plied between this point and Portland, laden with
lumber and firewood.   A trip in one of these
coasters is said to have inspired a high officer of
the college with the beneficent idea of writing a
book of " Songs for Sailors."   Though the little
volume fell still-born from the press, a few copies escaped, and gave occasion for great fun to
the irreverent youngsters, who parodied it with-

out mercy. I can only rescue for a brief hour
from oblivion the initial stanza of the first poem in
the book, and here offer it as a " specimen brick " :

> " All you who would be seamen
>   Must bear a valiant heart,
> And when you come upon the sea
>   You must not think to start ;
> Nor once to be faint-hearted
>   In hail, rain, wind, or snow ;
> Nor to think for to shrink
>   When the stormy winds do blow."

In process of time it was my fortune to "come
upon the sea," and I experienced the full force of
" hail, rain, wind, or snow " on several occasions
—notably in the *Portsmouth*, beating round Cape
Horn in a wild, wintry gale ; and again in the *Saratoga*, in a blinding storm of snow and sleet, embayed off the coast of New Hampshire, and only
saved from total shipwreck by cutting away the
masts and anchoring on a rocky lee-shore. I
take shame upon myself for, not recalling, then
and there, those appropriate and inspiriting lines.

To this little bay within a bay we occasionally
resorted, but the tiresome walk over the sandy
road deprived the excursions of half their pleasure.

The bay and the rapid river gave to the flat
region adjacent to the college its only picturesque
features. Of these Longfellow wrote :

> " Thou river, widening through the meadows green
>   To the vast sea, so near and yet unseen !"

―――

Another of our favorite strolls was in a sparse-
ly settled street by the riverside. There, after
tea, Hawthorne and I often walked, silent or
conversing, according to the humor of the hour.
These rambles sometimes ended at the unpainted
cottage of an old fortune-teller who, from the tea-
leaves in a cracked cup or from a soiled pack
of cards, evoked our respective destinies. She
always gave us brilliant futures, in which the
most attractive of the promised gifts were abun-
dance of gold and great wealth of wives. Lovely
beings these wives of destiny were sure to be,
some of whom the old crone prophesied would
be "dark-complected" and others "light-com-
plected," but all surpassingly beautiful. These
blessings, and more, she predicted for so small
a silver coin that, though we were her best pa-
trons, our modest stock of pocket-money was not
inconveniently diminished by her fees.

We were fully repaid for the outlay by the fun
of the hour ; but, to the discredit of the prophet-
ess, it must be said that the gold never came to
us, but to each a very happy marriage without
the dangerous procession of blondes and bru-
nettes. And it was an added tie between us

that each had the highest appreciation of the many excellent qualities of his friend's wife.

A few years since I revisited the spot where the sibyl once had lived; but, alas! only to find that her house was gone, and that a railway-track had usurped its former site.

———

In our long evening walks, especially when discussing the probable future of each, Hawthorne was less reserved than at other times. On such occasions I always foretold his success if he should choose literature as a profession. He listened without assenting, but, as he told me long afterwards, he was cheered and strengthened in his subsequent career by my enthusiastic faith in his literary powers.

The professors and students all acknowledged his superiority in Latin and English composition, yet to me he insisted that he could never bring himself into accord with the general reading public, nor make himself sufficiently understood by it to gain anything more than a beggarly support as an author. It was this distrust of being rightfully appreciated that, for so many years, prevented him from taking that rank among the foremost writers of America which scholars and critics now concede to him.

CHAPTER III.

THE class of 1825 became distinguished in the annals of Bowdoin for those of its graduates of that year who ultimately attained high rank in literature, theology, and politics.

Though the general reader may care little for any notice of the different individuals of this class, Bowdoin men will probably be interested in some account of its more noticeable members.

One of the youngest was Henry W. Longfellow, who entered college when only fourteen. He had decided personal beauty and most attractive manners. He was frank, courteous, and affable, while morally he was proof against the temptations that beset lads on first leaving the salutary restraints of home. He was diligent, conscientious, and most attentive to all his college duties, whether in the recitation-room, the lecture-hall, or the chapel. The word "student" best expresses his literary habit, and in his intercourse with all he was conspicuously the gentleman.

His studious habits and attractive mien soon led the professors to receive him into their society almost as an equal, rather than as a pupil; but this did not prevent him from being most popular among the students. He had no enemy.

Going forward for half a century after graduation, during which interval we met occasionally, but always cordially, the semi-centennial celebration of our class occurred, when he pronounced his famous poem, "Morituri Salutamus." At that reunion Longfellow was the central figure by reason of his eminence as a poet and scholar, his great culture, and his charming manners. The promise of the boy was more than fulfilled in the mature man.

Four years later I visited Longfellow on an interesting errand. The home of Miles Standish, at Duxbury, was burned the year before the "great Captain's" death; but the old cellar, filled with *débris*, was not thoroughly explored until a few years ago, when Mr. Drew, of Duxbury, and another gentleman gave much labor to its excavation. Among the articles found was a hoe, of such antiquated pattern as to leave no doubt of its having been used by the early Puritan. Mr. Drew was a great admirer of Longfellow, to whom he wished to send his Standish relic. Knowing that I was the poet's classmate, Mr. Drew begged me to convey the implement to him, which I did soon afterwards. Longfellow was pleased with the quaint offering, and at once

2

acknowledged its receipt in the following courteous note :

"CAMBRIDGE, August 23, 1879.

"DEAR SIR,—My friend and classmate, Bridge, has been here and brought me your valuable present. It is a curious relic of the past, and I like to think that the hand of the brave old Puritan has often held it, and plied it in the cornfield. Be assured that I value it very highly, and fully appreciate your kindness in presenting it to me, who have only a poetic claim to such a gift.

"With many thanks, yours very truly,

"HENRY W. LONGFELLOW.

"LYMAN DREW, Esq., Duxbury, Mass."

It was on this occasion that I last saw Longfellow. And, in reverting to my early acquaintance with the attractive boy of fourteen, it was pleasant to know that he had always been growing—intellectually and spiritually—until our parting at the age of more than threescore and ten.

Another of the remaining members of the class was Rev. Dr. George B. Cheever (the early and able leader in the cause of abolition and temperance), who attained high eminence as a theologian. Though one of the youngest of the students at Bowdoin, he was from the beginning very studious, and ambitious to excel as a scholar and writer. In character, conduct, and literary attainments he stood deservedly among the fore-

most.   His death in 1890 left but four of the
class alive.

Rev. Dr. John S. C. Abbott began his collegiate life with the definite purpose of entering
the ministry, and he subsequently became a
preacher of acknowledged ability in the Congregational Church.   After a few years, however, he
turned his attention to general literary work;
and, as author of several biographies and other
books, he had a reasonably successful career.
While at college, he was industrious in his studies
and exemplary in his habits, but he there took no
leading place as a profound scholar or brilliant
writer.

James W. Bradbury, one of the best scholars
in the class, became a well-known lawyer; and he
at one time represented Maine in the United
States Senate with ability and credit.

Three others of our classmates—Cilley, Ben-
son, and Sawtelle—were afterwards members of
the United States House of Representatives.

Cilley early gained a commanding position in
the national councils; and his future was full of
promise, when he fell in a duel with Graves, of
Kentucky, whose challenge he accepted rather
than be driven from his place, or be disgraced in
the eyes of those of his fellow-Congressmen who
held to the so-called "code of honor."   A political conspiracy by prominent Whigs to put the

brilliant young Democrat out of the way, or to destroy his influence, was successful, and Cilley was sacrificed to the ruthless demands of party. The following extract is from a letter that a United States Senator addressed to me on the day of Cilley's funeral, February 27, 1838: "Cilley was too promising and too independent to be allowed to remain in the way of the Whigs; and his death is the result of more deep and general policy than has been, and perhaps may ever be, made public."

As to the attributed influence of Hawthorne's example upon Cilley in the matter of his fatal duel with Graves, there is, I think, great misapprehension in some of the notices of that tragic event.

It was my fortune to be in Washington a month after Cilley's death, and to join the mess to which he had belonged. It was customary, at that period, for members of Congress to live in messes made up of political and personal friends. In one of these, on Third Street, were Senators Williams, of Maine; Pierce, of New Hampshire; and Wall, of New Jersey, with ladies of their respective families. At the suggestion of Mr. Williams and General Pierce, I was admitted to the mess, and I had the room that Cilley had so recently occupied. Of course I heard much of the origin and circumstances of the duel from the best authority.

It was charged by his opponents that General J. Watson Webb had changed the political character of his paper (*The Courier and Enquirer*) for a stated sum ($52,000). This transfer Cilley animadverted upon severely in debate, and for this General Webb sent him a challenge by Graves, of Kentucky. Cilley declined the challenge. Then Graves demanded that Cilley should say that he did so by virtue of his privilege as a Member of Congress (not to be accountable for words spoken in debate), and that he considered General Webb to be a gentleman. Upon Cilley's declining to make these admissions, Graves sent him a challenge by Governor Wise, of Virginia. To this Cilley replied that he had no controversy with Mr. Graves, whom he respected highly; but he refused to be catechised as to what he had said of Webb. Mr. Graves insisted upon the disavowal first demanded; and then Cilley, finding that the Whigs were determined to drive him to the wall, accepted Graves's challenge, and the tragic result followed.

The controversy was political, not personal, leading members of both parties consenting to and advising as to the course pursued by challenger and challenged respectively.

I never heard, at that time nor afterwards, that Cilley was in any way influenced by Hawthorne's example. Nor did Hawthorne himself

ever intimate to me, by word or letter, that he
considered himself at all responsible for Cilley's
course in accepting Graves's challenge.

One of Hawthorne's most intimate friends was
our classmate and my chum, William Hale, of
Dover, afterwards a merchant of high standing
and sterling integrity.

Another classmate and friend was Stephen
Longfellow, a lad of great wit and natural genius;
but, lacking the studious habits of his younger
brother, Henry, he gained no high rank in college, nor afterwards in the legal profession.

There was also Edward Preble, only child of
the renowned commodore, a boy of quaint humor
and fond of curious literature, who, after graduation, led a life of learned ease in Germany and
in his luxurious home in Portland, where he died
early without distinguishing himself, as he well
might have done had his ambition been com-
mensurate to his talents and his advantages.

Josiah S. Little, a man of high character and
great ability, who took the first honor in the class
after a severe struggle, was another instance of
the "young man's curse of competence." He
practised law for a few years, then quit the profession, and gave his attention to local politics
and the care of his large property, and he died
without achieving any wide national reputation.

Gorham Deane stood next to Little for scholarship. He was excessively studious. He allowed
himself but four hours for sleep, and took very
little exercise. Consequently his consumptive
tendencies developed into the illness that ended
his life a few weeks before the Commencement,
at which he would have graduated number two.
The empty honor of a degree eluded his grasp ;
but the trustees and overseers, by special vote,
inserted his name in the triennial catalogue as
having actually graduated.

Alfred Mason, Hawthorne's chum, was the son
of the distinguished lawyer Jeremiah Mason. He
was a youth of noble and generous nature, who
gained the esteem and respect of his fellows by
his courteous bearing and exceptional ability.
He devoted his efforts to the pursuit of natural
science in preference to the routine studies, and
after graduation engaged with enthusiasm in the
study and practice of medicine. At the outset
of a promising career he fell a victim to fever,
at the early age of twenty-four, while performing
his duties as assistant physician in Bellevue Hospital.

For myself it may be permissible to add that,
after practising law for a few years, I embarked
in a "great enterprise," as Americans would call
it ; to wit, the building a mill-dam across the
Kennebec River, with the hope of seeing many

mills and factories thereon, and of gathering in the gold predicted by the faithless old fortune-teller. The adventure turned out disastrously, for, after completing the work at a cost three times as great as the original estimate, a freshet — higher, of course, "than was ever before known"— swept away the dam and the mills, cut a new channel for the river, swallowed up our paternal mansion and grounds near by, and ruined me financially. I entered the navy as paymaster; and after sixteen years' service was made Paymaster-General of the navy, which office I held for fifteen years, including the whole period of the civil war.

Others of our number might be mentioned, but the class of 1825 will in future years be remembered mainly for having given to literature two such writers as Longfellow and Hawthorne.

———

Our associations were not confined to our own class. During the period from 1821 to 1825 inclusive this "country college" contained among its students, besides those just mentioned, John Appleton, afterwards the learned Chief Justice of Maine, and James Bell, United States Senator, of New Hampshire, both of the class of 1822; William P. Fessenden and Luther V. Bell, of 1823; President Pierce and Professor Calvin E. Stowe, of 1824. Later—in the class of 1826—came Sargent S. Prentiss, the brilliant orator of Mississippi, a native of Maine ; and John B. Russwurm, Governor of Cape Palmas, Africa. The class of 1827 contained Alpheus Felch, Governor and United States Senator, of Michigan ; and John P. Hale, United States Senator, of New Hampshire.

It is a noteworthy fact that one small class of thirty-eight—in a country college not a quarter of a century old—had among its members a romance writer and a poet, whose names stand among the foremost, each in his own branch of American literature.

The four classes (including our own) in college when we were freshmen, contained, at graduating, but one hundred and eight students in the aggregate ; yet among them there were not only the writers just alluded to, but also a future President of the United States and four United States Senators—a creditable record for any college, however large.

Here it may be well to mention that Fessenden, while in college, was ardent, haughty, and defiant. Warm in his friendships, he was bitter and uncompromising in his hatreds. He was a good writer and an excellent debater, and he took high rank as a scholar. In later life he stood among the foremost in the United States Senate ; and his leading position was readily conceded to him by his peers, in the trying times preceding and during the civil war.

Franklin Pierce, in the class next above ours, had many friends in our own, including Hawthorne, Cilley, and myself. These friends and others Pierce always remembered, even when occupying the highest place in the nation and burdened with its cares and responsibilities.

Indeed, he seemed to have much satisfaction in promoting the welfare and advancement of his college friends. To Hawthorne he gave the most lucrative foreign office in his gift, and I take pleasure in acknowledging that soon after his inauguration he — unsolicited — directed my recall from a foreign station, and appointed me to the highest place in my corps. I have reason to know that he never regretted his friendly course in either case.

It were foreign to the purposes of the present sketch to attempt an extended notice of President Pierce's life and character. Hawthorne's "Life of Franklin Pierce" gives an authentic biography of him previous to his elevation to the Presidency in 1852. His career afterwards is matter of history, and should be judged in the light of that day rather than by the changed conditions brought about by later national events.

I trust it will not be out of place for me to

give my own early impressions of Pierce's character, and my recollection of his appearance in
youth.

In person he was slender, of medium height,
with fair complexion and light hair, erect, with a
military bearing, active, and always bright and
cheerful. In character he was impulsive, not
rash; generous, not lavish; chivalric, courteous,
manly, and warm-hearted; and he was one of
the most popular students in the whole college.

The sketch of him in Professor Packard's " History of Bowdoin College " gives the following account of his standing as to scholarship and of
his indomitable spirit, as shown in correcting the
habits of idleness into which he had fallen, and
in retrieving his early mistakes in that respect.

" In 1820 Franklin Pierce," says his old teacher, " entered Bowdoin College. He was then sixteen years old. As yet he had formed no literary
tastes or habits of study, and the first half of his
college career was idled or played away. But he
suddenly woke up to a sense of duty to a true
manhood. When the relative standing of the
members of the class was first authoritatively ascertained in the junior year, he found himself occupying precisely the lowest position in point of
scholarship. In the first mortification of wound-
ed pride he resolved never to attend another rec-
itation, and accordingly absented himself from

college exercises for several days, expecting and
desiring that some form of punishment, such
as suspension or expulsion, would be the result. The faculty of the college, however, with
a wise lenity, took no notice of his behavior;
and at last, having had time to grow cool, and
moved by the grief of his friend Little and another classmate, Pierce determined to resume the
routine of college duties. 'But,' said he to his
friends, 'if I do so, you will see a change.' Accordingly, from that time forward he devoted
himself to study. His mind, having run wild
for so long a period, could only be reclaimed by
the severest efforts of an iron resolution; and,
for three months afterwards, he rose at four in
the morning, toiled all day over his books, and
only retired at midnight, allowing himself but
four hours for sleep.

"From the moment when he made his resolution until the close of his college life he never
incurred a censure; never was absent but from
two college exercises, and then unavoidably;
never went into the recitation-room without a
thorough acquaintance with the subject to be recited, and finally graduated the third scholar of
his class."

Pierce's classmate Calvin E. Stowe was a man
of mark in college, and was universally esteemed
and respected. He was an untiring student and

a deeply religious man, yet full of wit and quaint humor, which he strove to subordinate to his graver thoughts, that he might the better qualify himself for the important life-work in which he so eminently excelled. It was doubtless an heretical opinion, but when Mrs. Stowe's great work, "Uncle Tom's Cabin," first appeared, I felt confident that my old friend had lent a hand in the humorous portions of that wonderful book.

Stowe, though usually calm and unruffled, did, on rare occasions, show that the old Adam in his nature could be provoked to wrath. In my freshman year, prompted by the spirit of good-natured mischief, I blackened my face one night, and assuming the air of deference befitting a colored messenger-boy, I entered Stowe's room holding out a letter. He was deeply engaged with a book, but he rose to receive the letter, remarking, "Oh, it is from Mr. ——," at the same time taking out a piece of money to pay me for my trouble. This unexpected boon so upset my gravity that I laughed outright. Stowe was first surprised, then provoked by my impertinence, and he seized the tongs and cried, "You black rascal!" Whereupon I beat a hasty retreat, closing the door behind me just in time to escape the tongs, which came clashing against my guardian shield.

I think that Stowe did not suspect me, for we never spoke of the silly prank for more than fifty

years. But after that long interval, having received a kind message from him, asking me not
to pass through Hartford without calling, I went
to see him, and we had a pleasant talk about old
times. Then I made my tardy confession, to
which Mrs. Stowe was an amused listener, and
she seemed to enjoy hearing this proof of her
husband's ebullition of temper in his early manhood, which I thought it safe to divulge after
the lapse of so many years.

Governor Russwurm—the first and only colored graduate of Bowdoin, except in the medical
department—was a diligent student, but of no
marked ability. He lived at a carpenter's house,
just beyond the village limits, where Hawthorne
and the writer called upon him several times, but
his sensitiveness on account of his color prevented him from returning the calls. Twenty
years later I renewed the acquaintance pleasantly in Africa, where—as Governor of Cape
Palmas—he received, with dignity and ease, the
Commodore and officers of our squadron, myself
all the more cordially because we had been college associates and fellow-Athenæans.

John P. Hale, it is hardly necessary to say, was
one of the earliest and ablest advocates of abolition in the United States Senate, fighting its
battles fearlessly and almost alone for several
years. He was not studious in college, but, by

his remarkable talents and his great natural ap-
titude for learning, he maintained a respectable
rank in his class. He was distinguished mainly
for his ready wit, his great fund of anecdote, his
genial disposition, and his kind heart.

I mention these men in this cursory manner,
at the risk of being tedious, and chiefly to show
that Hawthorne, when in college, had around him
many students who, in after years, attained honorable distinction and place.

CHAPTER IV.

As to his social life in Brunswick, it may be said that Hawthorne, coming, as he did, from a family of exceptionally recluse habits, gained there his first practical knowledge of the world. It was not strange, therefore, that in his personal relations he formed few intimacies and rarely sought the friendship of others. Reserve was a prominent trait in his character, but it was the reserve of self-respect, not of pride or timidity. He discouraged advances in a negative way, and gave his confidence only to a few.

College friendships then, as now, were greatly influenced by association in the different literary societies. There were two of these at Bowdoin, the Peucinian and its young rival, the Athenæan. Several of the professors and most of the conservative students belonged to the first, while "Young Bowdoin" was more strongly attracted to the other.

The poet Longfellow was a Peucinian, and his elder brother an Athenæan. For that reason Hawthorne was better acquainted with Stephen

than with Henry, but the college relations of
the poet and the romance writer were always
kindly, and led to a strong friendship in later life.

———

Hawthorne was not studious in the general ac-
ceptation of the term, but he devoted much time
to miscellaneous reading. His facility for ac-
quiring knowledge would, with little labor, have
placed him in the front rank of his class. As it
was, he took much greater interest in the humani-
ties than in the more abstruse branches of the
prescribed course. Mathematics and metaphysics, as studies, he disliked and neglected, to his
frequent discredit in the recitation-room ; but the
languages were attractive and pleasant. Especially did he like the Latin, which he wrote with
great ease and purity. In the other studies of
the curriculum he stood hardly above medioc-
rity, and in declamation he was literally *nowhere.*
He never declaimed in the old chapel, as the
students were required to do on Wednesdays.
Fines and admonitions were alike powerless. He
would not declaim. To this peculiarity is to be
attributed his failure to have a part assigned him
in the Commencement exercises on graduation,
though his rank, No. 18 in a class of thirty-eight,
would otherwise have entitled him to one.

He told me that when twelve or thirteen years

3

old, on some occasion in play-hours, he went upon a stage in the school-room to declaim. Some larger boys ridiculed him and pulled him down, which so mortified and enraged him that he was inspired with a lasting aversion to any future effort in that direction. Nor did he attempt to speak in public until many years afterwards, when, as United States Consul at Liverpool, he made a speech at a civic dinner, of which he wrote me an amusing account. He was more exultant at his success on that occasion than he ever seemed to be for the authorship of " The Scarlet Letter."

In the literary aspirations of his collegiate life poetry had apparently no place. Yet some small poems of his — written before entering college, and still resting in my memory—showed, as I thought, considerable merit. Since, however, he refrained from writing verses afterwards, one can only conjecture what his success would have been had he made poetry instead of prose the vehicle for his fancies.

In the " Biography," and in Mr. Lathrop's " Study," it appears that, while a young boy, he was much addicted to rhyming. At sixteen, however, he wrote his sister, " I have almost given up writing poetry. No man can be a poet and a book-keeper at the same time." This was written when he expected to become a merchant. For, in the same letter, he wrote, " I do not think

I shall ever go to college. I cannot bear the thought of living upon Uncle Robert for four years longer. How happy I should be to be able to say, 'I am lord of myself.' "

The world may well bless the memory of "Uncle Robert," that his liberality was unfaltering, and that his estimate of the judicious course for his nephew's education was so correct. Little, though, did he dream of the inestimable benefit he was bestowing upon all English-speaking peoples by his wise expenditure for the future author's training.

Reverting to the subject of poetry, I believe there is no evidence of Hawthorne's writing any poetry after he entered college, though he frequently quoted it. Apropos to his ante-college versifying, I remember that, on a moonlight evening, Hawthorne and I were leaning over the railing of the bridge just below the falls, listening to the falling water, and enjoying the beauties of the scene, when I recited some passages from the colloquy between Lorenzo and Jessica in the "Merchant of Venice." Then Hawthorne, in his deep, musical tones, responded with the following verses, which he said he had written before coming to college :

" We are beneath the dark blue sky,
  And the moon is shining bright.
Oh, what can lift the soul so high
  As the glow of a summer night,

When all the gay are hushed to sleep,
And they who mourn forget to weep
    Beneath that gentle light?

" Is there no holier, happier land
    Among those distant spheres,
Where we may meet that shadow band,
    The dead of other years,
Where all the day the moonbeams rest,
And where at length the souls are blest
    Of those who dwell in tears?

"Oh, if the happy ever leave
    The bowers of bliss on high,
To cheer the hearts of those who grieve,
    And wipe the tear-drop dry,
It is when moonlight sheds its ray,
More pure and beautiful than day,
    And earth is like the sky."

I preserved the lines, and a few years since gave a copy to Mr. Lathrop, who published them in his interesting " Study of Hawthorne."

I remember also another little poem of Hawthorne's, which I wrote down soon after hearing it, but the manuscript was lost.   It ran thus:

" The ocean hath its silent caves,
    Dark, quiet, and alone;
Though there be fury on the waves,
    Beneath them there is none.

" The awful spirits of the deep
    Hold their communion there,
And there are those for whom we weep—
    The young, the brave, the fair.

" The earth hath guilt, the earth hath care,
  Unquiet are its graves,
But peaceful sleep is ever there
  Beneath the dark blue waves.

" Calmly the wearied seamen rest
  Beneath their own blue sea ;
The ocean's solitudes are blest,
  For there is purity."

This little poem was afterwards set to music by E. L. White.

CHAPTER V.

HAWTHORNE, previous to entering college, lived in great seclusion with his mother and two sisters at their home in Salem. In two or three flying visits, made him by invitation after our graduation, I saw no evidence of narrow circumstances in their environment. I was charmed with the quiet and refined manners of Mrs. Hawthorne and with the pleasant and lady-like bearing of her younger daughter. The elder daughter—who Hawthorne often said had more genius than himself—I never saw until after his death.

The family occupied the old home of Mrs. Hawthorne's father, their moderate income being sufficient for their comfortable support, but not for the son's college expenses. These had been defrayed by his maternal uncle, Robert Manning, who supplied him with means to spend as liberally as any of his companions.

In these days of more costly education it may interest some readers to know the simpler college expenses of sixty or seventy years ago. A

term bill of my own, yellow with age, dated
May 23, 1823, is before me, and contains these
items :

For tuition..........................	$8	00
Chamber rent.......................	3	34
Damages............................		45
Average damages....................		15
Sweeping and bed-making............	1	11
Library.............................		50
Monitor............................		05
Catalogues.........................		08
Bell...............................		11
Reciting-room......................		25
Chemical lectures...................		25
Fines		20
Total......................	$14	49

The fines were probably for absence from rec-
itations ; but a later term bill shows a fine of
twenty-five cents for " unnecessary walking on
the Sabbath," a charge that would astonish the
father of any collegian of the present day.   Could
Hawthorne's term bill of corresponding date be
found, it would doubtless show that he, too, was
convicted of the misdemeanor of taking a stroll
after our compulsory attendance at morning and
afternoon services.

In a corner of the present campus stood
" Ward's tavern " when I first went to Bruns-

wick. Its owner had recently died, and was
succeeded in his vocation by his daughter, a
maiden of perhaps thirty years—affable, good-
looking, and always ready to give moderate
credit for the little suppers and other comforts
that students might desire. Her house was the
scene of many social gatherings; but at some
later period it disappeared, and the grass of the
college grounds now conceals the site of that
once most convenient inn. There, oftener than
elsewhere, Hawthorne indulged in the usual con-
vivialities of the period; but his sedate aspect
and quiet manners prevented the appearance of
any excess, even within the limited circle of his
intimate associates. The customary pastimes
included card-playing and wine-drinking, in
which he joined his friends through good fellow-
ship; but he rarely exceeded the bounds of mod-
eration—never losing more money than he could
readily pay, and never imbibing enough to ex-
pose himself to remark. He could drink a great
deal of wine without, apparently, being affected
by it. Neither in his college days nor afterwards
did I ever know him to be perceptibly under the
influence of stimulants, though we were associated in many convivial scenes. I will add that,
from the first moment of our acquaintance, I
never knew him to utter an unmanly sentiment
or to do a mean or unkind act.

In our last term, after the parts for the Commencement exercises had been assigned, it appeared that fourteen of the thirty-eight graduates of the year were not to have the privilege of " speaking in public on the stage," though their degree of A.B. was nevertheless to be conferred. This rear-guard rallied and formed " The Navy Club," so called for some occult reason. It comprised among its members a future Congressman, another who in the course of time became a reverend D.D., Hawthorne, and, of course, the writer.

Of the officers elected, the D.D. was made Commodore, Hawthorne was Commander, myself Boatswain, and the most fun-loving of the party was designated Chaplain. Every one had a title, from Commodore to Cook.

The weekly suppers at Miss Ward's were very jolly; and some of the class, who, by reason of superior standing as scholars, were not entitled to membership would fain have joined in the merry sessions of the club, but they were not admitted.

The nightly meetings of Commencement week ended this drama, as well as many others of more grave import.

The river near by gave its name to a loo club of five members. One died early, but not until he had achieved political fame of a high order;

another was afterwards a wealthy and respected merchant ; a third became a physician and settled in the West, where he was held in high regard until he died, thirty years ago. Hawthorne and the writer were the other members of the Androscoggin Club, which existed about two years. The stakes played for were, of course, small, but the golden hours then lost were not included in the account.

That Hawthorne was somewhat addicted to card-playing quite early in his college life appears from a letter of President Allen to Mrs. Hawthorne, May 29, 1822 (see "Study," p. 117), announcing the fact that her son had that day been "fined fifty cents for playing cards for money last term."

That dignitary adds, " Perhaps he might not have gamed, were it not for the influence of a student whom we have dismissed from college."

The next day Hawthorne himself writes his mother, "All the card-players in college have been found out—my unfortunate self among the number. One has been dismissed from college, two suspended, and the rest, with myself, fined fifty cents each."

By good fortune I was not caught in that grand raid, but several men who afterwards attained eminence—e. g. a U. S. Senator, a grave judge, and a leading physician—were included, with Hawthorne, in the "catch."

———

It may be interesting to Bowdoin men to know where Hawthorne lived while in college.

At first he and Mason boarded at Professor Newman's, and had their room in Maine Hall, where they remained until the building was burned in March, 1822. Fortunately they were upon the lower floor, so they easily saved their furniture and other effects.

Soon afterwards Hawthorne wrote his sister, " I sustained no damage by the fire except having my coat torn. Luckily it happened to be my old one."

After this enforced removal the two room-mates took up their quarters in the large house of Mrs. Adams, opposite the president's house. This most estimable lady—the widow of a leading physician—had been left with two charming daughters and only moderate means of support. Hence it was convenient, as it was in accordance with the custom of the place, to utilize three or four rooms in her large house by renting them to students.

A year or two later I occupied a room in the same house, and we incidentally noticed, with mild interest, the attentions a young medical student was paying to the elder daughter of the house. Soon afterwards they married and went West.

The sequel to the story came fifty-five years later, when I found myself at table, in a Washington hotel, with a dignified Western Representative and his lady-like wife and pretty daughter. Their name had a familiar sound, and soon the fact dawned upon me that I was talking with the son of my old Brunswick friends, in the person of the prominent and able Colonel Hatch, of Missouri.

The college youth (now a gray-haired veteran) and the young maiden (now a venerable widow) who had bidden good-by in 1825 were able, in 1880, to exchange messages of regard across half a continent.

Returning from this digression, it remains only to be added that, after Maine Hall had been rebuilt Hawthorne and Mason returned to it, and occupied room No. 19 in the sophomore year.

For the last two years in college, Hawthorne roomed alone at Mrs. Dunning's, directly opposite Professor Cleveland's house, where also we both boarded. The cost of board was moderate, and we fared satisfactorily for a sum that would now seem inadequate, and even mean. Two dollars a week was the highest charge for table-board, and most of the students paid but a dollar and a half.

Hawthorne and the writer usually lived at the same boarding-house and were quite contented with the fare. The incidental expenses of college were small, but even such of the rooms as were uncarpeted and uncurtained were not cheerless, for wood was abundant at a dollar a cord. The one comparatively large item of expense (excepting books and stationery) was that of the "midnight oil," which was brought from a village "store" and burned in brass or japanned lamps. After so long an interval—especially as gas and electric light have come into use—no harm can follow from divulging the secret that certain students had extra lamp-fillers that had never known oil. And these were carried in broad daylight across the campus, full of some other liquid more quickly and pleasantly consumed.

Maine had not then enacted the laws which have given her such creditable prominence as the pioneer in the cause of temperance. At that time, too, it was the universal custom for country stores to sell "wines and liquors" as well as "dry-goods and groceries."

———

Hawthorne engaged in the usual college sports, but with no great zest. Base-ball and foot-ball interested him little, though he occasionally joined

in the rough-and-tumble games.   He did not like
running or jumping, but walking was his favorite
exercise ; in that he was untiring.   Sometimes he
went out shooting, though he did not claim to be
a crack shot.   I never saw him on horseback, but
frequently of a Saturday we drove in the "chaise"
or in the wagon of that day, he never wishing to
hold the reins.

CHAPTER VI.

ALTHOUGH Hawthorne, while a collegian, rarely sought or accepted the acquaintance of the young ladies of the village, he had a high appreciation of the sex. An early marriage, however, did not enter into his plans of life. The evidence of this fact is among my papers and runs thus:

"BOWDOIN COLLEGE, Nov. 14, 1824.

"If Nathaniel Hathorne is neither a married man nor a widower on the fourteenth day of November, One Thousand Eight Hundred and Thirty-six, I bind myself upon my honor to pay the said Hathorne a barrel of the best old Madeira wine.

"Witness my hand and seal.

"JONATHAN CILLEY."

[J. C.]

"BOWDOIN COLLEGE, Nov. 14, 1824.

"If I am a married man or a widower on the fourteenth day of November, One Thousand Eight Hundred and Thirty-six, I bind myself, upon my honor, to pay Jonathan Cilley a barrel of the best old Madeira wine.

"Witness my hand and seal.

"NATHANIEL HATHORNE."

[N. H.]

"This instrument shall be delivered to Horatio Bridge, and if Hathorne is married within the time specified, he shall transmit the intelligence to him immediately, and the bet, whoever shall lose it, shall be paid within a month after the expiration of the time.

"JONATHAN CILLEY,
"NATHANIEL HATHORNE."

This very formal agreement was enclosed in a closely sealed package, endorsed in Hawthorne's writing, thus:

"Mr. Horatio Bridge is requested to take charge of this paper, and not to open it until the fifteenth day of November, 1836, unless by the joint request of Cilley and Hathorne."

On the designated day I broke the seals, and notified Cilley that he had lost the wager. He admitted the loss and, after the delay of a year or more, was making arrangements for its payment and a meeting to taste the wine, when his tragic death, in the duel with Graves, settled the account.

Many years ago Hawthorne requested me to
burn the letters he had written me in his youth
and early manhood.   On reading them over, I
found them full of passages of beauty and of details of his own plans and purposes, hopes and
disappointments.   They were, however, too free
in their expressions about persons and things to
be safely trusted to the chances of life; and all
his early letters were destroyed.   Many of these
were signed "Oberon," and others the familiar
"Hathorne" or "Hath."

In a letter of Miss Peabody, quoted by Mr.
Conway, it is stated that "his classmates called
Hawthorne 'Oberon the Fairy' on account of
his beauty, and because he improvised tales." It
seems a pity to spoil so poetic a fancy; but, if
truthful narrative is required, the cold facts are
these:

In reality the pseudonym of "Oberon" was
not given to him by his classmates or by any
one else while in college, but was assumed by
him at a later date and in this wise.   Soon after
graduation we agreed to correspond regularly at
stated periods, and we selected new signatures
for our letters.   Hawthorne chose that of "Oberon" (which he afterwards used for some of his
magazine articles), while I took the more prosaic
one of "Edward."

Neither his beauty nor his improvised tales

4

had anything to do with his sobriquet of "Oberon."

While in college and for some years afterwards he spelled his name without the *w*. On first seeing the improved signature I wrote him that it was suggestive of a fat legacy, to which he replied that he had been blessed with no such luck, though he would gladly take every letter in the alphabet for a thousand dollars each. He added that, in tracing the genealogy of his family, he had found that some of his ancestors used the *w*, and he had merely resumed it.

Later, he sometimes took the signature of "L'Aubépine," which name he adopted temporarily, in accordance with the whim of a queer Frenchman who spent a month with us in my bachelor home in Maine, as described in the "American Note-Books," Vol. I., p. 49. There Hawthorne says: "He has Frenchified all our names, calling B——, Monsieur Du Pont; myself, M. de L'Aubépine; and himself, M. de Berger; and all Knights of the Round Table."

There was a musical society at Bowdoin, though not many of the students were instrumental performers. Longfellow played the flute, but Hawthorne was notably deficient in musical talent. Like Charles Lamb, he might have said, "The gods have made me most unmusical."

CHAPTER VII.

The faculty of Bowdoin College was respectable, ranking probably as high as that of any other young college—the time here spoken of being within the first quarter of a century of its existence.

The president had been a Congregational minister, and was a man of piety, doubtless. He was precise in dress, and his gait—whether in summer's heat or winter's cold—was always methodical, measured, and slow.

He was vigilant in securing the legal rights of the college and in promoting its material interests. He was industrious and conscientious; but his manner was precise and formal, instead of being dignified; and he inspired the average student with little respect or esteem.

Professor Cleveland, the oldest and, by far, the most distinguished member of the faculty, had few if any superiors in the country as geologist or chemist. He was as kind and genial as he was learned. He took a fatherly interest in the students who applied themselves in earnest to the branches of study in his department, and he regarded "more in sorrow than in anger" those who failed to show a proper appreciation of their advantages in this respect. Outside his own lecture-room he had little to do with collegiate discipline, unless it were to give his voice in favor of leniency to some luckless culprit. Never was professor held in higher regard, nor could any one have inspired more kindly respect.

Professor Newman first filled the chair of Ancient Languages and afterwards that of Rhetoric and Oratory. He was courteous, refined, and scholarly; yet he was swift-footed and prompt to detect and bring to grief innocent lads enjoying their little amusements, such as lighting bonfires, smashing tutors' windows, burning powder in various ways, etc.

" Haud inexpertus loquor."

Professor Smythe, the mathematical professor, had few friends in our set. Whether from want of tact in the teacher or from inaptitude in the scholar, we usually associated the professor with the abhorred conic sections and algebraic solutions which he strove to inject into our unreceptive brains. Although recognizing his ability, we too often failed to meet his requirements. For the rest, he was learned in his specialty and exact in the performance of his duties, and he possessed great zeal and energy withal.

Professor Upham, in our senior year, was Professor of Moral and Mental Philosophy. He was young, scholarly, gentle, and kind to the students, by all of whom he was much beloved.

Professor Packard was tutor and, afterwards, Professor of Latin. He was studious, sympathetic, and very handsome. He only of the faculty survived at the time of our class semi-centennial, and he died in 1884. Longfellow, in delivering his poem of " Morituri Salutamus " at that celebration, turned and addressed the revered professor thus :

> " They are no longer here, they all are gone
> Into the land of shadows—all save one.
> Honor and reverence and the good repute
> That follows faithful service as its fruit
> Be unto him whom, living, we salute."

Thirteen of the thirty-eight graduates of the class at the time of that reunion were living, eleven of whom were present.

Rev. Dr. George B. Cheever was the class orator and Longfellow the class poet. Seated together upon the stage, the eleven gray-haired men presented a striking contrast to the young graduates before them, who, " with the sublime audacity of faith," were just starting out upon the race of life that we had so nearly run. The veterans who had separated fifty years before, full of vigor and confidence, had returned to the once familiar scenes, and, after half a century of vicissitudes, had come to take their final leave of Bowdoin.

On the next day Rev. Dr. J. S. C. Abbott gave a history of the class in detail, correct in the main, but quite too flattering to the majority.

The class had several meetings during the Commencement season. The last was held on the campus, quietly and without publicity. Beneath the " Liberty Tree," with the sun shining down from a cloudless sky, the little band stood around the tree and listened reverently to a solemn benediction from Rev. Dr. Shepley, and then, with mutual wishes of " God bless you " and " Farewell," parted to meet no more on earth.

But three of the thirteen graduates survive at the present writing, in 1892. " The fatal asterisk of Death " is set against the names of the others.

Before separating we all agreed to interchange our photographs. In making the exchange, Longfellow wrote to me thus:

" CAMB., Dec'r 12, 1875.

" MY DEAR BRIDGE,—I have just had the pleasure of receiving your photograph. It is so good, it could hardly be better. I wish the one

I send you in return were as good. But that is wishing that I were a handsome man, six feet high, and we all know the vanity of human wishes.

"I was very glad that you and Mrs. Bridge were not disappointed in Songo River and its neighborhood. If "Long Pond" were called Loch Long, it would be a beautiful lake. This and Sebago are country cousins to the Westmoreland lakes in England, quite as lovely, but wanting a little more culture and good society.

"I often think with great pleasure of our meeting at Brunswick. There was less sadness about it than I had thought there would be. The present always contrives to crowd out the past and the future.

"With kindest remembrances to Mrs. Bridge,
        "Always yours,
            "HENRY W. LONGFELLOW."

The whole letter is copied because — while speaking of the class reunion—the poet incidentally gives his estimate of Sebago Lake, on the borders of which Hawthorne spent a year of his lonely boyhood, and to which locality he refers when he says, "It was there I first got my cursed habit of solitude."

Hawthorne visited Brunswick but once to meet his old associates. It was in 1852—fifty years after the founding of the college. In that year, while cruising in the Pacific, I received a letter from him, in which he says :

" I meant to have told you all about my visit to Brunswick at the recent semi-centennial celebration, but the letter has already grown to too great length. It was rather a dreary affair. Only eight of our classmates were present, and they were a set of dismal old fellows, whose heads looked as if they had been out in a pretty copious shower of snow. The whole intermediate quarter of a century vanished, and it seemed to me as if they had undergone a miserable transformation in the course of a single night, especially as I myself felt just about as young as when I graduated. They flattered me with the assurance that time had touched me tenderly, but alas ! they were each a mirror in which I beheld the reflection of my own age. I did not arrive there until the public exercises were nearly over, and very luckily too, for my praises had been sounded by orator and poet, and, of course, my blushes would have been quite oppressive."

———

In a desultory and inartistic way I have thus endeavored to throw some additional light upon Hawthorne's college life and his surroundings at that period. At the risk of repetition, I will add that his most marked characteristics were independence of thought and action; absolute truthfulness; loyalty to friends; abhorrence of debt; great physical as well as moral courage; and a high and delicate sense of honor.

He shrank habitually from the exhibition of his own secret opinions, and was careful to avoid infringement upon the rights of others, while thoroughly conscious of his own.

On closing our college association, we mutually pledged our friendship and exchanged parting gifts. Hawthorne's to me was a watch-seal of his father's, gold with a carnelian stone, of the shape and fashion of ninety years ago. I have treasured it carefully, and have provided that it shall go to his son at my decease.

A brass hand lies upon my desk, holding the several sheets of paper as I write. It was presented by me to Hawthorne at some time before I first went to sea in 1838; and—after his death in 1864—it was given back to me by Mrs. Hawthorne, with the information that it had been habitually used by Hawthorne to hold the loose papers on his table. It will soon go back (like the watch-seal) to one of his children.

———

Of my own intimacy with Hawthorne I have

hitherto said little, having been content with the mention made of it by my friend in his published writings; and I trust it will not be thought presumptuous that I have jotted down here some reminiscences that incidentally show our strong friendship, while rounding out the story of his college life.

CHAPTER VIII.

THE narrative of Hawthorne's life after leaving college has been published in his own "Note-Books," edited by Mrs. Hawthorne ; in the able biography of "Nathaniel Hawthorne and his Wife," by their son ; and in the interesting "Study of Hawthorne," by his son-in-law ; to say nothing of the sketches of the romance writer by Fields, Curtis, Stoddard, James, and others. But though the principal facts—essential to a biography—have been given in those publications, and however much may have been written upon this subject, there remain unrecorded many incidents, the recital of some of which may be acceptable to those readers who prize every fresh fact concerning this author of superlative power and fame. I may therefore hope that my ample knowledge of his personal, political, and literary character will enable me to add something worthy of record to the mass of facts that go to make up the story of his life. My contribution will at least have the value of personal recollections. To these I am able to add many interesting letters of Hawthorne and his wife.

If, at any time, I should repeat what has already been published by others, except for the purpose of commenting upon or of giving some additional facts pertinent thereto, the repetition will be unintentional.

I am not a critic, and therefore shall not venture upon an analysis of Hawthorne's writings—a task which many pens abler than mine have already essayed, and which critics yet unborn will doubtless contribute to the literature of the future. Nor shall I attempt to write a biography of the romance writer—a work already accomplished in the publications just mentioned. These were admirable, each in its way ; and recently they have been supplemented by the " Life of Nathaniel Hawthorne," by Moncure D. Conway, a volume I have read with much interest, though he seems to me to have been quite too severe and unjust in his criticism of Hawthorne for having written the " Life of Franklin Pierce " and for his own opinions on the subject of slavery. Had Mr. Conway known the charm of Pierce's warm-heartedness and his devoted friendship for Hawthorne he could have better understood that it would have been hard for the latter to withhold the use of his voice and pen in promoting the interests of his early friend.

If Mr. Conway had regarded the problem of disunion as did all parties, except the pronounced abolitionists, previous to the civil war, he might have been more charitable in his judgment of both Pierce and Hawthorne.

It should be remembered that before the war broke out the Northern Democrats and a large portion of the Republicans considered the preservation of the Union in its entirety as of paramount importance, and were not willing to jeopardize it by plunging the country into war, though they looked upon slavery as a deplorable evil. They had been educated to believe that the Constitution was sacred and binding upon all the States—North and South—and that no State had the right to repudiate the contract into which all had entered.

No Northern man had better means of knowing the dangers impending, previous to the outbreak of the war, than had General Pierce. Intimately associated—as he was—with the strong men of the South, in his Cabinet and in Congress, he saw that the Southerners were determined, at all hazards, to defend their peculiar institution of slavery, which was imperilled by the abolitionists. While the Northern Republicans in general scouted the idea that the Slave States would go to war with such odds in men, money, and war-material against them, Pierce knew that the South was in dead earnest.

Northern men, in position to see the signs of the times, were strangely obtuse to them. Shortly before South Carolina seceded I was at table in Washington with a Republican Congressman from Central New York, when a Northern lady, who had exceptional means of knowing the true state of Southern feeling, earnestly assured him that the South would certainly secede unless the prevailing excitement could be allayed. The Congressman smiled and said, " Mrs. ——, I will give you a hundred dollars for each State that secedes, and a hundred for every day it stays out." It goes without saying that had the pledge been kept, the lady would have been in much more prosperous circumstances than she is in to-day.

In the Senate, when the Southern Senators, one after another, made their impassioned protests against the course of the Republicans, most of the Northern Senators listened in unconcealed incredulity, not believing that the warnings could be serious; but Pierce saw the dangers of the crisis, and would have gone far and suffered much to avert them. He did not love slavery, but he tolerated it rather than see the Union destroyed.

For weal or for woe, he was always true to the Constitution and the Union.

———

Probably the first visit of more than a day or two that Hawthorne ever made (outside his own family circle) was one to me in my bachelor quarters in Augusta, Maine, in 1837.

My paternal home—a spacious house of twenty rooms—had come into my possession by inheritance; and, as my brothers and sisters had all gone to new homes after our father's decease, I was left sole occupant of the mansion, with the exceptions of my factotum Tom and a family who lived in a wing of the building and attended to the housekeeping.

I had given a room to my French teacher (an odd Franco-German from Alsace) that I might utilize my spare hours by improving my knowledge of French.

To this irregular household Hawthorne came to spend a month with me; and doubtless it was a pleasure to him—as it certainly was a great one to me—that we could thus enjoy a few weeks' reunion, without ceremony and without restraint.

The Frenchman's vocation took him away for the daytime, but he returned at night to amuse and enliven us by his gayety, his philosophy, and his eccentricities.

This queer foreigner was, to Hawthorne, an object-lesson which he did not fail to improve, as his journal shows. Some of the entries in that journal bring out, in strong relief, one prominent trait in his character. I mean that of noticing, critically, all scenes and incidents worthy to be remembered, and of jotting down some of his observations for future use.

His mental sight was both panoramic and microscopic; and he looked at persons and things with a discerning and discriminating eye, whether the object of his attention were a friend or a stranger—a tree or a flower—a hill or a pebble. Thus he dissected the character and described the personality of the French teacher with a lenient, yet impartial hand, while he portrays him in this manner:

"Mons. S—— does not appear to be more than twenty-one years old—a diminutive figure, with eyes askew, and otherwise of an ungainly physiognomy; he is ill-dressed also, in a coarse blue coat, thin cotton pantaloons, and unbrushed boots; altogether with as little French coxcombry as can well be imagined, though with something of the monkey aspect inseparable from a little Frenchman. He is, nevertheless, an intelligent and well-informed man, apparently of extensive reading in his own language—a philosopher and an infidel.

*   *   *   *   *

"The little Frenchman impresses me very strongly too—so lonely as he is here, struggling against the world, with bitter feelings in his breast and

yet talking with the vivacity and gayety of his nation—making this his home from darkness to daylight, and enjoying here what little domestic comfort and confidence there is for him ; and then
going about all the livelong day, teaching French
to blockheads who sneer at him, and returning at
about ten o'clock in the evening to his solitary
room and bed. Before retiring, he goes to B——'s
bedside, and if he finds him awake stands talking
French and expressing his dislike of the Americans—' Je hais, je hais les Yankees !' thus giving
vent to the stifled bitterness of the whole day.
In the morning I hear him getting up early—at
sunrise or before—humming to himself, scuffling
about his chamber with his thick boots, and at
last taking his departure for a solitary ramble
till breakfast. Then he comes in, cheerful and
vivacious enough, eats pretty heartily, and is off
again, singing French *chansons* as he goes down
the gravel-walk. The poor fellow has no one to
sympathize with him but B——, and thus a singular connection is established between two utterly different characters.

"Then there is myself, who am likewise a queer
character in my way, and have come to spend
a week or two with my friend of half a lifetime—
the longest space probably that we are destined
to spend together ; for Fate seems preparing
changes for both of us. My circumstances, at

5

least, cannot long continue as they are and have been; and Bridge, too, stands between high prosperity and utter ruin."

The "Twice-Told-Tales," had just been published, but Hawthorne had not then gained full confidence in the favorable effect of the publication upon his future prospects; and, to myself, the "utter ruin" came, a few months later, in the destruction of the expensive dam and mills, on the successful outcome of which I had staked all that I possessed.

My own time was engrossed by affairs, and I saw little of my French guest except in the early morning and at night, when he came back to us as to friends in whom he could find the sympathy and appreciation which so rarely came into his isolated life. Without influence and without means—of obscure parentage and grotesque personality, yet with a good education—he had come to América, seeking the fortune and distinction which he could not hope for in his native home.

Hawthorne's visit (all too soon for me) came to an end; and shortly afterwards the Frenchman —having finished his teaching in the village— went away to "seek pastures new," and I saw him no more. Hawthorne had returned to the seclusion of his home, and the French waif went, by invitation, to spend a few days in Salem, where a ludicrous incident occurred to the two companions.

They were strolling one day through the fields near Salem, when—not noticing the yellow flag of warning—they passed within the precincts appropriated to a small-pox hospital and were at once made prisoners by the custodians of this place for the infected, and were not liberated until they had been fumigated by burned leather and subjected to other disinfectants. This tyrannous treatment doubtless—and with good reason—brought out the little Frenchman's emphatic cry of " Je hais, je hais les Yankees "; but Hawthorne enjoyed the *contretemps* immensely.

———

In the first decade after Hawthorne left college he formed several plans of life, one of which was that of entering his Uncle Manning's counting-house. In one of his letters to me he spoke of this as a settled purpose, but his repugnance to commercial life was such that the plan was ultimately abandoned, and he relapsed into the state of partial inaction which so often results from unsettled plans.

It is well known that, soon after graduating, he prepared for the press a little volume of tales, entitled " Seven Tales of my Native Land." The publisher who engaged to bring out the book was so dilatory that at last Hawthorne, becoming impatient and dissatisfied with the excuses given, peremptorily demanded the return of the manuscript. The publisher, aroused to a sense of his duty and ashamed of his broken promises, apologized and offered to proceed with the work at once; but Hawthorne was inexorable; and though, as he wrote me at the time, he was conscious of having been too harsh in his censures, he would not recede, and he burned the manuscript, in a mood half savage, half despairing. As I expressed to him—perhaps too strongly—my regret for this proceeding, he did not, when "Fanshawe" was published, confide to me the fact. Hearing, though, of the publication, I procured a copy, and subsequently mentioned it to Hawthorne. He had meantime become dissatisfied with the book, and he called in and destroyed all the copies he could reach. At his request I burned my copy, and we never alluded to "Fanshawe" afterwards. It was at this time, I think, that he became utterly disheartened, and, though conscious of possessing more than ordinary literary talent, he almost abandoned all expectation of success as an author.

In one of his letters to me, after relating some of his disappointments, he compared himself to one drifting helplessly toward a cataract, and closed with these despairing words, "I'm a doomed man, and over I must go."

Happily the despondent mood was not per-

NATHANIEL HAWTHORNE

After a Painting by C. G. Thompson, 1850

manent, and he continued to write, though subjected to frequent disappointments. He was a
contributor for a little while to a magazine published, I believe, in New York. The compensation was small, and even that the publisher
professed his inability to pay. So Hawthorne
stopped his contributions and withdrew.

At the parting a characteristic incident occurred. The editor begged for a mass of manuscript in his possession, as yet unpublished, and
it was scornfully bestowed. "Thus," wrote Hawthorne, "has this man, who would be considered
a Mæcenas, taken from a penniless writer material incomparably better than any his own brain
can supply." And he closed with a bitter male-
diction upon the grasping editor.

He had the experience of being more than
once deceived by those who professed to have
the power and wish to befriend him. A young
man, with some means and greater aspirations,
commenced the publication of a literary newspaper in Boston, and offered him the position of co-
editor. Another person, backed by a rich father,
supplanted Hawthorne, who was civilly bowed
out, and the newspaper, after a brief and sickly
life, expired.

In the Hawthorne Biography there appeared
several old and carelessly written letters of my
own — answers to some of Hawthorne's that
were, long since, destroyed at his request.

These letters I should hardly have reproduced except for the purpose of showing that Hawthorne was at times quite despairing and in need of all the encouragement his friends could give.

The following extracts from my answers, just mentioned, will indicate sufficiently the tenor of his letters therein referred to :

"AUGUSTA, Oct. 16, 1836.

"DEAR HATH,—I have a thousand things to say to you, but can't say more than a hundredth part of them. . . .

"You have the blues again.   Don't give up to them for God's sake and your own, and mine, and everybody's.   Brighter days will come, and that within six months. . . .

"See what I have written for the Boston *Post*, and tell me is it best to send it?

"'It is a singular fact that, of the few American writers by profession, one of the very best is a gentleman whose name has never yet been made public, though his writings are extensively and favorably known.

"'We refer to Nathaniel Hawthorne, Esq., of Salem, the author of the "Gentle Boy," the "Gray Champion," etc., etc., all productions of high merit, which have appeared in the annuals and magazines of the last three or four years.

"'Liberally educated, but bred to no profession, he has devoted himself exclusively to literary pursuits, with an ardor and success which will, ere long, give him a high place among the scholars of this country.

" ' His style is classical and pure ; his imagination exceedingly delicate and fanciful, and through all his writings there runs a vein of sweetest poetry.

" ' Perhaps we have no writer so deeply imbued with the early literature of America ; or who can so well portray the times and manners of the Puritans.

" ' Hitherto Mr. Hawthorne has published no work of magnitude ; but it is to be hoped that one who has shown such unequivocal evidence of talent will soon give to the world some production which shall place him in a higher rank than can be obtained by one whose efforts are confined to the sphere of magazines and annuals.'

" This is not satisfactory by any means ; and yet it may answer the purpose of attracting attention to your book when it comes out. It is not what I wish it were, nor can I make it so.

" Yours ever,

" H. BRIDGE." *

---

* This letter was written at the time when I had just intervened to procure the publication of " Twice-Told-Tales,"

"AUGUSTA, Oct. 22, 1836.

"DEAR HATH,—I have just received your last, and do not like its tone at all. There is a kind of desperate coolness about it that seems dangerous. I fear that you are too good a subject for suicide, and that some day you will end your mortal woes on your own responsibility.

"However, I wish you to refrain till next Thursday, when I shall be in Boston, *Deo volente*.

"I am not in a very good mood myself, just now, and am certainly unfit to write or think.

"Be sure you come and meet me in Boston.

   "Yours truly, H. BRIDGE."

"AUGUSTA, Dec. 25, 1836.

"DEAR HAWTHORNE,—On this Christmas day I am writing up my letters. Yours comes first.

"I am sorry that you did not get the magazine, because you wanted it. Not that I think it very important to you. You will have more time for your book. . . .

"Whether your book will sell extensively may be doubtful; but that is of small importance in

---

without Hawthorne's knowledge of my agency in the matter.

Within the six months' limit the book came out, and brighter days did come ; but I could not then tell him the grounds of my confident prediction.

the first one you publish. At all events, keep up
your spirits till the result is ascertained; and,
my word for it, there is more honor and emolument in store for you, from your writings, than
you imagine. The bane of your life has been
self-distrust. This has kept you back for many
years; which, if you had improved by publishing, would long ago have given you what you
must now wait a short time for. It may be for
the best, but I doubt it.

"I have been trying to think what you are so
miserable for. Although you have not much property, you have good health and powers of writing, which have made, and can still make, you
independent.

"Suppose you get 'but $300 per annum' for
your writings. You can, with economy, live upon
that, though it would be a tight squeeze. You
have no family dependent upon you, and why
should you 'borrow trouble'?

"This is taking the worst view of your case
that it can possibly bear. It seems to me that
you never look at the bright side with any hope
or confidence. It is not the philosophy to make
one happy.

"I expect, next summer, to be full of money,
a part of which shall be heartily at your service,
if it comes. . . .

"And so Frank Pierce is elected Senator.

There is an instance of what a man can do by
trying. With no very remarkable talents, he at
the age of thirty-four fills one of the highest sta-
tions in the nation. He is a good fellow, and I
rejoice at his success. He can do something for
you perhaps. The inclination he certainly has.
Have you heard from him lately?

"Yours ever,   H. BRIDGE."

"AUGUSTA, Feb. 1, 1837.

"DEAR HAWTHORNE, — So your book is in
press, and will soon be out. Thank God the
plunge will be made at last. I am sure it will
be for good. . . .

"I coincide perfectly with you touching the
disparity between a writer's profits and a pub--
lisher's. It *is* hard that you should do so much
and receive so little from *The Token*. You say
an editorship would save you. I tell you that
within six months you may have an editorship in
any magazine in the country if you desire if. I
wish to God that I could impart to you a little of
my own brass. You would then dash into the
contest of literary men, and do honor to yourself
and to your country in a short time. But you
never will have confidence enough in yourself,
though you will have fame. . . .

"Yours truly,

"HORACE."

" AUGUSTA, May 24, 1837.

" DEAR HAWTHORNE,—I am rejoiced that your last gives me reason to expect that you will pay me a visit soon. When you come, make your arrangements so that you can stay two or three months here. I have a great house to myself, and you shall have the run of it.

" I received a letter two days ago from Pierce, dated May 2d, requesting me to ascertain exactly how matters were relating to the exploring expedition. I have written Pierce, advising him to inquire of the Secretary of the Navy if there is any vacancy, and recommending you for it.

" It might be well to put your papers on file in his office, in case you should be a candidate for one of the editorships of the magazine.

" It is of no use for you to feel blue. I tell you that you will be in a good situation next winter instead of 'under a sod.' Pierce is interested for you, and can make some arrangement I know. An editorship or a clerkship at Washington he can and will obtain. So courage, and *au diable* with your 'sods!'

" I have something to say to you upon marriage and about Goodrich, and a thousand other things. I shall be inclined to quarrel with you if you do not come, and that will be a serious business for you, for my wrath is dreadful. Good-by till I see you here.   Yours truly,   H. BRIDGE."

These letters in some measure indicate the despondency to which Hawthorne was subjected at this, the turning-point in his literary career. In his secluded life he neither had nor sought new friends who could have aided and encouraged him, and his life wore away with little apparent promise. Still he continued to write for the small sums he received in cash or promises as well as for the pleasurable excitement of composition and with the growing hope of future success.

CHAPTER IX

BESIDES writing tales for different reviews and magazines, Hawthorne contributed many articles to *The Token*, an annual published by Mr. S. G. Goodrich. A few years later he was employed by that publisher to write some of the " Peter Parley" books. He received but small compensation for any of this literary work, for he lacked the knowledge of business and the self-assertion necessary to obtain even the moderate remuneration vouchsafed to writers fifty years ago. It would be amusing, if it were not exasperating, to observe the patronizing tone of Mr. Goodrich, when, as late as September, 1836, he wrote to Hawthorne, " Your letter and the two folios of 'Universal History' were received some days ago. I like the history pretty well. I shall make it do." See " Biography of Hawthorne," Vol. I., p. 138. The book certainly *did*, for its sale went above a million long ago, though it is my impression that the author received only $100 for the work.

A letter of S. G. Goodrich to Hawthorne,

dated January 19, 1830—see "Hawthorne Biography," Vol. I., p. 131—shows that Mr. Goodrich had then in his hands the manuscript of a proposed book of Hawthorne's. He says in relation to it, "On my return to Boston in April, I will use my influence to induce a publisher to take hold of the work, who will give it a fair chance of success."

In a letter of Hawthorne's to Goodrich, dated May 6, 1830, given in Derby's "Fifty Years among Authors and Publishers," p. 113, the former speaks of the "Provincial Tales," adding, "Such being the title I propose to give to my volume."

Whatever may have been the causes for delay, the fact remains that the volume, under the altered title of "Twice-Told-Tales," did not appear until 1837—seven years after the manuscript—in part—was first in Mr. Goodrich's possession.

From time to time I heard of this intended publication, and constantly encouraged Hawthorne to bring out the volume. But I hesitated to intervene without his sanction, and that would not have been given to any course involving possible loss to me. At last, however, having become convinced that my friend was being deluded by false hopes, I wrote to Mr. Goodrich and asked if there was any pecuniary obstacle in the way of the publication ; adding, if that were the cause of the delay, I would obviate it by guaranteeing the publisher against loss. As I was a stranger to him, I proffered Boston references. The following was his answer :

"BOSTON, Oct. 20, 1836.

"DEAR SIR,—I received your letter in regard to our friend Hawthorne. It will cost about $450 to print 1000 volumes in good style. I have seen a publisher, and he agrees to publish it if he can be guaranteed $250 as an ultimate resort against loss. If you will find that guaranty, the thing shall be put immediately in hand.

"I am not now a publisher, but I shall take great interest in this work; and I do not think there is any probability that you will ever be called upon for a farthing. The generous spirit of your letter is a reference. I only wish to know if you will take the above risk. The publication will be solely for the benefit of Hawthorne; he receiving ten per cent. on the retail price—the usual terms. I am, yours respectfully,

"S. G. GOODRICH.

"HORATIO BRIDGE, Esq., Augusta, Me."

I gave the requisite guaranty at once, stipulating only that the affair should be concealed from Hawthorne; for I was sure he would object to the publication if he were informed of my action

in the premises.   Mr. Goodrich assented to this
stipulation, and in due time the book came out.

There is reason to suppose that he magnified
his own part in the matter, for, while the volume
was going through the press, Hawthorne told me
that he intended to dedicate it to Mr. Goodrich,
in recognition of his services in that regard.

Knowing that this would bring the parties into
a false attitude towards each other, I cautioned
Hawthorne against this proposed dedication, as
appears in a forgotten letter of mine, published
in the "Hawthorne Biography," Vol. I., p. 143.
Having learned from Mr. Goodrich — some
months after "Twice-Told-Tales" appeared—
that its sales had satisfied the guaranty, I told
Hawthorne of my unauthorized intervention, as
it was clearly right that he should know the extent of his obligation to the publisher.

The letter of Mr. Goodrich, just quoted, will
interest some readers, as showing the cost of
printing books, and the comparative avails to author and publisher, in 1836.   The retail price of
"Twice-Told-Tales" was, I believe, one dollar.
From the $1000 first obtained, after deducting
the cost of printing ($450) and the author's share
($100), there would remain to the publisher and
the retail bookseller $450.   For any copies print-
ed in excess of the first thousand, the cost to the
publisher would be much less, while the author's

percentage would remain the same. This in a case where the publisher was assured against loss. How different would have been Hawthorne's encouragement had he commenced his literary work in this decade!

The success of "Twice-Told-Tales" was not pecuniarily great at first, but in this country and still more in England, where Hawthorne was promptly and highly appreciated, the book established his right to a place among living authors of recognized power.

The cloud had lifted at last, and he never afterwards wholly despaired of achieving success as a writer. There were times, however, when he felt unequal to the effort of writing even a letter, saying that he "detested a pen."

Fortunately his habits were inexpensive, and his abhorrence of debt nerved him to retain his independence in the darkest seasons.

Several letters of my own (hereinbefore given, and quite forgotten until they appeared in the "Hawthorne Biography") show that I was constantly advising him to cease publishing in magazines and annuals, and to bring out his writings in the form of volumes only. By this method he could free himself from the necessity of offering his productions piecemeal to editors—a process repulsive to his sensitive spirit.

6

Early in 1837 General Pierce, believing that Hawthorne would be benefited by an entire change of his surroundings, suggested to him the plan of joining the contemplated Exploring Expedition to the South Sea as its historian. The project pleased him, and for three or four months an active correspondence relating to this subject was maintained by Hawthorne, Pierce, and the present writer. Several letters of General Pierce and myself—addressed to Hawthorne and published in the " Hawthorne Biography," pp. 152 to 162—refer to the efforts made to bring about the desired arrangement.

This expedition was primarily organized under the plan of J. N. Reynolds, Esq.—a man of some scientific reputation and great energy of character —who was to be the ruling spirit of the enterprise. ·

A squadron under the command of Commodore Ap Catesby Jones, composed of the frigate *Macedonian*, three brigs, and a store-ship, was put in commission for this exploring duty; and a large scientific corps, with Reynolds at its head, was provided for.

At that time I was spending the winter in Washington, and I did what I could to secure for Hawthorne the office he desired. My friend and townsman, Hon. R. Williams, was Chairman of the Senate Naval Committee, and, of course, was influential at the Navy Department. He cordially co-operated with Pierce and Cilley, backed by the rest of the Maine and New Hampshire delegations, in the effort to secure Hawthorne's appointment. With the influences at work there was a good prospect of success, when naval and scientific jealousy interrupted the programme.

The cry of economy was raised, the vessels were ordered to other duty, and Reynolds's ambitious project suddenly collapsed so far as he was concerned.

The expedition was reorganized the next year, and Lieutenant — afterwards Rear - Admiral — Wilkes was ordered to its command. Meantime Hawthorne's prospects had brightened with the success of " Twice-Told-Tales," and he ceased to care for duty in the expedition.

Had his aspirations in that direction been successful the current of his life would have been strangely disturbed, and his later writings would, I think, have taken on an entirely different coloring—whether for the better, who shall say?

In 1839 Hawthorne was appointed weigher and gauger in the Boston Custom-house, which office he held until 1841. Thus two years of his life were devoted to the routine duties of an office requiring only the practical qualities possessed by men of ordinary intelligence and reliability; and he brought his good sense to bear upon his prosaic duties, which he performed faithfully and well. On leaving the custom-house he joined the colony at Brook Farm, where he lived for several months as co-laborer, and especially as an interested inquirer into the social experiment then and there in progress. He had previously become engaged to Miss Sophia A. Peabody, and this episode was tentative as to the expediency of making the Farm a temporary home for his intended wife and himself. But his pecuniary interest in the scheme was that of creditor, not partner. He loaned Mr. Ripley $1000 or $1500, which money, when closing his connection with the association, he was unable to recover without resorting to legal measures, which he did through the agency of G. S. Hillard, Esq., with what ultimate result I do not know.

I drove out from Boston two or three times to see Hawthorne at Brook Farm. He had a small room, simply furnished, and with very few books visible. He was apparently enjoying himself, curiously observing the odd phase of life around him, and, while having little faith in the success of the social experiment, doing his full share to secure it. At the same time, he was disposed to get such amusement as he might from his surroundings. I remember that he boasted of hav-

ing driven into Boston with the farmer in the
farm-wagon, wearing a linsey-woolsey frock, and
carrying a calf to market.

I remember also his glee in telling of his strictly enforcing the rules for early rising by blowing
the horn—long and loud—at five o'clock in the
morning, much to the discomfort of the drowsy
members of the family. But enough of Brook
Farm. It has been fully chronicled in many
publications.

CHAPTER X.

IMMEDIATELY after his marriage, in 1842, Hawthorne went to reside in the "Old Manse" at Concord, where his life for three years was restful and happy. Full of enjoyment in his home and family, he was only troubled by narrow means, which was all the more annoying because those who owed him money enough to make life comfortable would not (doubtless some of them could not) pay their debts. In this quiet retreat he occupied himself in writing tales, gardening, boating, and occasionally in receiving friends.

Several times Mr. and Mrs. Hawthorne kindly urged me to visit them at the "Old Manse," and I was always received with the most cordial hospitality. Their life at Concord has been so fully and so beautifully described by Mr. Julian Hawthorne in the biography of his father and mother —not only in his own narration, but in their charming letters therein given—that it is perhaps needless for me to add anything to that recital. Let me say, however, that I was early impressed with the conviction that their marriage was a con-

THE "OLD MANSE"

genial and most happy one. By the delicate
health of Mrs. Hawthorne she was all the more
endeared to her manly husband, and in return
she gave him a wealth of confidence, admiration,
and love. The union was most fortunate for both,
and the only drawback to their happiness came
in the sharp economy requisite for living within
their income.

The small and uncertain receipts from his literary work, as well as his "disappointments in
money expected from three or four sources,"
made Hawthorne "sigh for the regular monthly
payments at the custom-house," and led him to
wish for the Salem post-office, the appointment to
which his friends in that town and elsewhere
zealously, though in vain, sought to procure for
him.

In 1845 Hawthorne, besides preparing for the
press the second series of "Twice-Told-Tales,"
edited the "Journal of an African Cruiser."

The origin of that little volume was this: Early
in 1843 I was attached to a ship-of-war under
orders to the West Coast of Africa. Hawthorne
suggested the plan of my taking such notes as
would give me material for a few articles in the
Democratic Review. This plan was afterwards,
by his advice, changed to that of publishing the

notes in a book. I assented to the change on the condition that he should take the trouble of editing and bringing out the volume, and with the further condition that he should have the copyright and the sole profit of the publication.

The letters next following evince the great interest he took in this project—more on my account than on his own. They also set forth his views as to the best mode for successful journalizing, and they show conclusively that his life was a very happy one in the " Old Manse."

"CONCORD, March 24, 1843.

" DEAR BRIDGE,—I see by the newspapers that you have had the good fortune to undergo a tremendous storm.* Good fortune I call it, for I should be very glad to go through the same scene myself if I were sure of getting safe to dry land at last. I did not know of your having sailed, else I might have been under great apprehensions on your account ; but, as it happened, I have only to offer my congratulations. I hope you were in a condition to look at matters

---

* The storm here spoken of refers to a violent gale and blinding snow-storm off the coast of New Hampshire (as mentioned on an earlier page), in which the *Saratoga* (on her way from Portsmouth to New York, previous to the African cruise) was in imminent peril, and only escaped total shipwreck by our cutting away the masts and anchoring on a rocky lee-shore.

with a philosophic eye—not sea-sick nor *too much* frightened. A staff-officer, methinks, must be more uncomfortable in a storm than the sea-officers. Taking no part in the struggle against the winds and the waves, he feels himself more entirely at their mercy. Perhaps a description of the tempest may form a good introduction to your series of articles in the *Democratic*.

"I returned from my visit to Salem on Wednesday last. My wife went with me as far as Boston. I did not come to see you because I was very short of cash, having been disappointed in money that I expected from three or four sources. My difficulties of this sort sometimes make me sigh for the regular monthly payments at the custom-house. The system of slack payments in this country is most abominable, and ought, of itself, to bring upon us the destruction foretold by Father Miller. It is impossible for any individual to be just and honest and true to his engagements when it is a settled principle of the community to be always behindhand. I find no difference in anybody in this respect. All do wrong alike. —— is just as certain to disappoint me in money matters as any pitiful little scoundrel among the book-sellers. On my part I am compelled to disappoint those who put faith in my engagements, and so it goes round. The devil take such a system!

" I suppose it will be some time before you get to sea again, and perhaps you might find leisure to pay us another visit, but I cannot find it in my conscience to ask you to do so in this dreary season of the year. It is more than three months since we had a glimpse of the earth, and two months more must intervene before we can hope to see the reviving verdure. I don't see how a bachelor can survive such a winter. . . . We are very happy, and have nothing to wish for except a better filled purse—and not improbably gold would bring trouble with it, at least my wife says so, and therefore exhorts me to be content with little.

" I have heard nothing about the office since I saw you. They tell me in Salem that —— will not probably gain his election, but that after a few more trials a coalition will be formed between the moderate Whigs and the candidate of a fraction of the Democratic party. In that case —— will not get the post-office, and possibly it will yet be the reward of my patriotism and public services, but of this there is little prospect.

" The wine came safe, and my wife sends her best acknowledgments for it. As in duty bound, however, she has made it over to me, and I shall feel myself at liberty to uncork a bottle on any occasion of suitable magnitude. Longfellow is coming to see me, and as he has a cultivated taste in wines, some of this article shall be submitted to his judgment. If possible there shall be a bottle in reserve whenever you favor us with another visit.

"Do not forget your letters from Liberia. What would you think of having them published in a volume ? But it will be time enough for this after their appearance in the magazine. I should like well to launch you fairly on the sea of literature.

"I have a horrible cold, and am scarcely clearheaded enough to write. God bless you,

"NATH HAWTHORNE.

"HORATIO BRIDGE, Esq., U. S. N., Portsmouth, N. H."

"CONCORD, May 3, 1843.

"DEAR BRIDGE,—I am almost afraid that you will have departed for Africa before this letter reaches New York; but I have been so much taken up with writing for a living, and likewise with physical labor out-of-doors, that I have hitherto had no time to answer yours. It was perhaps as well that you did not visit Concord again, for by comparison of dates I am led to believe that my wife and yourself were in Boston at the same time. She had gone thither to take leave of her sister Mary, who is now married, and has sailed in the May steamer for Europe.

" I formed quite a different opinion from that which you express about your description of the storm. It seemed to me very graphic and effective, and my wife coincides in this judgment. Her criticism on such a point is better worth having than mine, for she knows all about storms, having encountered a tremendous one on a voyage to Cuba. You must learn to think better of your powers. They will increase by exercise. I would advise you not to stick too accurately to the bare fact, either in your descriptions or your narrative ; else your hand will be cramped, and the result will be a want of freedom that will deprive you of a higher truth than that which you strive to attain. Allow your fancy pretty free license, and omit no heightening touches because they did not chance to happen before your eyes. If they did not happen, they at least ought, which is all that concerns you. This is the secret of all entertaining travellers. If you meet with any distinguished characters, give personal sketches of them. Begin to write always before the impression of novelty has worn off from your mind, else you will be apt to think that the peculiarities which at first attracted you are not worth recording ; yet those slight peculiarities are the very things that make the most vivid impression upon the reader. Think nothing too trifling to write down, so it be

in the smallest degree characteristic. You will
be surprised to find on re-perusing your journal
what an importance and graphic power these
little particulars assume. After you have had
due time for observation, you may then give
grave reflections on national character, custom,
morals, religion, the influence of peculiar modes
of government, etc., and I will take care to put
them in their proper places and make them come
in with due effect. I by no means despair of
putting you in the way to acquire a very pretty
amount of literary reputation, should you ever
think it worth your while to assume the authorship of these proposed sketches. All the merit
will be your own, for I shall merely arrange them,
correct the style, and perform other little offices
as to which only a practised scribbler is *au fait.*

"In relation to your complaint that life has
lost its charm, that your enthusiasm is dead,
and that there is nothing worth living for, my
wife bids me advise you to fall in love. It is
a woman's prescription, but a man — *videlicet,*
myself—gives his sanction to its efficacy. You
would find all the fresh coloring restored to the
faded pictures of life ; it would renew your youth ;
you would be a boy again, with the deeper feeling and purposes of a man. Try it, try it—first,
however, taking care that the object is in every
way unexceptionable, for this will be your last

chance in life. If you fail you will never make another attempt.

"I suppose you will see O'Sullivan in New York. I know nothing about the prospects of office, if any remain. It is rather singular that I should need an office, for nobody's scribblings seem to be more acceptable to the public than mine; and yet I shall find it a tough scratch to gain a respectable support by my pen. Perhaps matters may mend; at all events, I am not very eager to ensconce myself in an office, though a good one would certainly be desirable. By the bye, I received a request the other day from a Philadelphia magazine to send them a daguerreotype of my phiz for the purpose of being engraved. O'Sullivan likewise besought my wife for a sketch of my head, so you see that the world is likely to be made acquainted with my personal beauties. It will be very convenient for a retired and bashful man to be able to send these pictorial representations abroad instead of his real person. I know not but O'Sullivan's proposal was meant to be a secret from me, so say nothing about it to him.

"It would gladden us much to have you here for a week, now that the country is growing beautiful, and the fishing season is coming on. But this is not to be hoped for until your return. Take care of your health, and do not forget the sketches. It is not the profit to myself that I think about, but I hope that they may contribute to give your life somewhat of an adequate purpose, which at present it lacks.

"God bless you.   N. H.

"HORATIO BRIDGE, Esq., U.S. Ship *Saratoga*, New York City."

"CONCORD, April 1, 1844.

"DEAR BRIDGE,—Your letter to my wife was received by her in a situation which I am sure you will consider sufficient excuse for her not answering it at present, a daughter having been born on the 3d of last month. So, you see, I am at last the regular head of a family, while you are blown about the world by every wind. I commiserate you most heartily. If you want a new feeling in this weary life, get married. It renews the world from the surface to the centre.

"I am happy to tell you that our little girl is remarkably healthy and vigorous, and promises, in the opinion of those better experienced in babies than myself, to be very pretty. For my own part, I perceive her beauty at present rather through the medium of faith than with my actual eyesight. However, she is gradually getting into shape and comeliness, and by the time when you shall have an opportunity to see her, I flatter myself she will be the prettiest young lady in the world. I think I prefer a daughter to a son.

"We have read your letter with very great interest. You have had great luck certainly in having actually fought through a whole war; but I hope that you will now be content to rest on your laurels.* The devil take those copper-slugs! As your station, I believe, does not call you to the front of the battle, do pray be advised to stay on board ship the next time, and think how much preferable is a sluggish life to such a *slug*-gish death as you might chance to meet on shore. A civilized and educated man must feel somewhat like a fool, methinks, when he has staked his own life against that of a black savage and lost the game. In the sight of God one life may be as valuable as another, but in our view the stakes are very unequal. Besides, I really do consider

---

* The "war" referred to in this letter hardly rose to the dignity of a skirmish, consisting, as it did, in the landing of a detachment of sailors and marines, with their officers, from the ships of the squadron, and the burning of five native villages. This destruction was effected for the purpose of punishing the natives for plundering and burning an American vessel and murdering the captain and the crew.

King Krako, the leader of these five tribes, showed fight, his men firing upon us from the woods, but doing no damage except the wounding of a marine with a copper slug, presumably made of a spike from the luckless *Mary Carver*.

the shooting of these negroes a matter of very questionable propriety, and am glad, upon the whole, that you bagged no game upon either of those days.

" In one point of view, these warlike occurrences are very fortunate—that is, in supplying matter for the journal. I should not wonder if that were your object in thrusting yourself into these perils. Make the most of them.

" If I mistake not, it will be our best plan, both as regards your glory and my profit, to publish the journal by itself, rather than in a magazine, and thus make an independent author of you at once. A little of my professional experience will easily put it into shape, and I doubt not that the Harpers, or somebody else, will be glad to publish it, either in the book or pamphlet form, or perhaps in both, so as to suit the different classes of readers. My name shall appear as editor, in order to give it what little vogue may be derived from thence, and its own merits will do the rest.

" You must have as much as possible to say about the African trade, its nature, the mode of carrying it on, the character of the persons engaged in it, etc., in order to fit the book for practical men. Look at things, at least some things, in a matter-of-fact way, though without prejudice to as much romantic incident and adventure as you can conveniently lay hold of. Oh, it will be an excellent book.

"I have no news to tell you except the great event with which I began my letter. I continue to scribble tales, with good success so far as regards empty praise, some notes of which, pleasant enough to my ears, have come from across the Atlantic. But the pamphlet and piratical system has so broken up all regular literature that I am forced to write hard for small gains. If we have a Democratic President next year I shall probably get an office. Otherwise, it is to be hoped, God will provide for me and mine in some other way.

"I have not written to you before, not from coldness nor forgetfulness, but partly because the sight of a pen makes me sick, and partly because I never feel as if a letter would reach you in your wanderings on the trackless ocean. If you had any certain abiding-place it would be different; but now it is like trying to shoot a bird in the air. Take care of yourself, and keep clear of night dews and copper slugs.

"Your friend, N. H.

"HORATIO BRIDGE, Esq., U. S. Ship *Saratoga*, African Squadron."

"SALEM, Nov. 29, 1844.

"DEAR BRIDGE,—I have just received your let-

.ter at this place, where we have been spending Thanksgiving.

"It heartily rejoices me to know that you are again on your native soil. I do not think I shall return to Concord for ten days or a fortnight; so that it is very possible we may meet in Boston.

"As to the post-office, ——'s kinsman is now out of the question. A new appointment was made two or three months ago, but it has not been confirmed by the Senate. As the removal was entirely on political grounds, there seems to be considerable doubt whether they will sanction it. Very probably your influence might cause the rejection of the new incumbent; in which case I think I might have a good chance for the office from Polk. The late appointment is not particularly satisfactory to the Democrats here, as the man belongs to the —— clique, which has never lost its influence in Essex County. If I am not misinformed, Tyler had actually appointed me, but was afterwards induced to change it. He will probably leave it to the next administration to make a new appointment.

"God bless you. If you come to Boston within a fortnight, let us know. Inquire at 13 West Street.   Yours ever,

"N. HAWTHORNE.
"HORATIO BRIDGE, Esq., Washington."

The three letters next following relate princi-. pally to the "Journal of an African Cruiser," which was published in 1845.

"CONCORD, April 17, 1845.

"DEAR BRIDGE,—I am happy to announce that your book is accepted, and will make its appearance as one of the volumes of "Choice Reading." Few new authors make their bows to the public under such favorable auspices; but you always were a lucky devil, except in the speculation of the Kennebec mill-dam, which, likewise, may turn out to have been good luck in the long run. I have christened the book the "Journal of an African Cruiser." I don't know when it is to come out—probably soon; although I suppose they will wish the American series to be led by some already popular names. Your last letter arrived when the manuscript was on the point of being sent off, but I contrived to squeeze in whatever was essential of the new matter.

"I have heard nothing—good or bad—as to the result of the P. O. application. Duyckinck, in his letter about the book, mentions that O'Sullivan was in Washington, where doubtless he will do all that can be done in my behalf. Your interview with Bancroft gave me better auspices than I before had on the subject.

"Mrs. Hawthorne wishes me to tell you that

she will not be able to make you the talked-of visit the approaching summer. Her sister, Mrs. Mann, is coming to board in Concord, principally with a view to being near Sophia, and even if I should obtain an office, I shall leave her here at the Old Manse for the summer and resume a bachelor-life in Salem. It shall go hard, but I will drop in upon you at least for a day or two, or for a dinner, if better may not be.

"Una continues to flourish. Her mother lulls her to sleep every night by stories about your visit, so that you were not only pleasant while here, but are very profitable now that you have departed. Your friend,

"NATH HAWTHORNE.

"HORATIO BRIDGE, Esq., Navy Yard, Portsmouth, N. H."

"CONCORD, May 2, 1845.

"DEAR BRIDGE,—Duyckinck writes me that your book is stereotyped and about to go to press. The first edition will be of two thousand copies, five hundred of which will be sent to London. It seems they have put in my name as editor, contrary to my purpose, and much to my annoyance; not that I am troubled with any such reluctance about introducing you as you felt about introducing your friend —— to fashionable society; but I wished you to have all the credit of the work yourself.   Well, you shall still engross all the merit, and may charge me with all the faults.

"I have bespoken fifty copies for you, and directed them to be sent to my address in Boston, whence I will take care to have them forwarded to you immediately, with the exception of perhaps half a dozen, which I shall reserve for distribution myself.   You had better send me the names of the persons whom you wish to have copies in Boston and vicinity.   The fifty copies will be paid for out of my avails for the book, for it would be rather too severe a joke to make your work an actual expense to you.

"I have heard nothing from O'Sullivan, nor from any other source, in reference to the post-office.

"Write forthwith and tell me how the books should be sent from Boston to Portsmouth.

"Your friend,

"NATH HAWTHORNE.

"HORATIO BRIDGE, Esq., Navy Yard, Portsmouth, N. H."

"CONCORD, May 7, 1845.

"DEAR BRIDGE,—I send the Journals as requested, and heartily wish that I could afford to come myself.   Have you told Charles Greene of the forthcoming book?   If not, it will be best to

do so immediately, that he may be in readiness
to add his voice to the general acclamation of
praise. I requested Duyckinck to send your
copies to Dr. Peabody's, directed to me. They
probably will not arrive so soon as this, but it
will do no harm for you to call there before leaving Boston, and if you find them, you can dispose
of them according to your pleasure, leaving out
six, or, if you can spare them, ten copies, which
I will endeavor to dispose of so as to promote
the interests of the book. If you find that you
have not copies enough, we can procure more
from New York.

" In a hurry, your friend,

"NATH HAWTHORNE."

"CONCORD, August 19, 1845.

" DEAR BRIDGE,—I have this moment received
your letter, and answer it in the post-office. I
know not whether you can do anything for us in
New York, but should be glad to have you call
on O'Sullivan. He has written me a letter which
my wife mailed for me at Salem after reading it,
but which has not yet reached me. It referred
to an offer by Bancroft of an office (a clerkship, I
suspect) connected with the Charlestown Navy
Yard—the salary $900. This offer I shall not
accept; and I wish you to tell O'Sullivan so,
and request him to inform Bancroft. Perhaps it

would be well to let O'Sullivan into the whole
business of our late canvass, so that he may be
aware of the strength with which we shall take
the field at the next session of Congress.

" Do come and see us on your return.

" In great haste

    " Your friend,

       " NATH HAWTHORNE.

" HORATIO BRIDGE, Esq., Astor House, N. Y."

CHAPTER XI.

In the autumn of 1845 the family left Concord and returned to Salem, in reference to which Hawthorne wrote:

"SALEM, Oct. 7, 1845.

" DEAR BRIDGE,—Here I am, again established in the old chambers where I wasted so many years of my life. I find it rather favorable to my literary duties, for I have already begun to sketch out the story for Wiley & Putnam. I received a letter from Duyckink to-day, which I mean to enclose as giving authentic intelligence of the welfare of your book.

"Your check arrived seasonably, and did me as much good as the same amount ever did anybody.

*   *   *   *   *

" Sophia has remained in Boston in order to see her friends in and about the city, before withdrawing into my den. I shall bring her

home the latter part of this week or the first of
next.   Your friend,

" NATH HAWTHORNE.

" HORATIO BRIDGE, Esq., U. S. Navy Yard,
Portsmouth, N. H."

" 20 CLINTON PLACE, Oct. 2, 1845.

" DEAR SIR, — I hope you will not think me
a troublesome fellow if I drop you another line
with the vociferous cry, MSS.! MSS.! Mr. Wiley's American series is athirst for the volume of
Tales, and how stands the prospect for the ' History of Witchcraft ' I whilom spoke of?

" The ' Journal of the Cruiser ' has just gone to
a second edition of a thousand copies, the first, I
believe, having been two thousand. W. & P. project cheap series of these books for the school
district libraries, in the first of which the Journal will be included.

" The English notices are bounteous in praise.
No American book in a long time has been so
well noticed.

" Pray, MSS. or no MSS., let me hear from you,
that you are well and your family.

" Yours truly,   EVERT A. DUYCKINCK.
" NATHANIEL HAWTHORNE, Esq."

" SALEM, Feb. 21, 1846.

" DEAR BRIDGE,—A day or two after receiving

your letter communicating the arrangement about the Surveyorship and Naval office, I had one from O'Sullivan who had been in Washington, but had just returned to New York. He appeared to know nothing about the above arrangement, but said that the President had promised to give me either the Surveyorship or Naval office. It appears therefore that I may consider myself pretty certain of getting one or the other, and I trust it will be the Surveyorship, which is the most eligible, both on account of the emolument and the position which it confers. Whichever it is, it is to you I shall owe it among so many other solid kindnesses. I have as true friends as any man; but you have been the friend in need and the friend indeed.

"In other respects, too, my affairs look promising enough. Wiley & Putnam are going to publish two volumes of my Tales instead of one, and I shall send off the copy, I hope, on Monday. My mind will now settle itself after the long inquietude of expectation; and I mean to make this a profitable year in the literary way.

"I regret that you are so soon thinking of going to sea again. You must not go without giving me the chance of another visit, though of the briefest duration.

"I hope, moreover, that you will remain ashore until I am again established in a home of my own, when it will be easy for you to be my guest often, at bed and board. We are neighbors now.

"Your friend,

"NATH HAWTHORNE."

I have found the following scrap of a letter which must have been written soon after my return from the coast of Africa, in 1845, since it refers to some furs known as African lynx, which I had brought home and presented to Mrs. Hawthorne.

The deep satisfaction he expressed in his wife and his—then—only child makes this fragment worth preserving.

"The skins came safe yesterday morning, and Sophia, I believe, contemplates having them made into a muff. She and Una are very well, and Una continues to talk about 'Misser Bidge.' After all, having a wife who thoroughly satisfies me, and a child whom I would not exchange for a fortune, I am not quite so unlucky a devil as you set me down for.   Your friend,

"NATH HAWTHORNE."

When Mr. Polk became President, the plan of campaign for Hawthorne's appointment to the Salem Post-office was pursued with vigor for a while; but there were strong political obstacles

in the way, and consequently his efforts and those
of his friends were turned towards the Surveyorship of the Salem Custom-house, an office of
less labor and responsibility, though of smaller
emolument than the post-office afforded.

Referring to a visit made me in the summer
of 1845, at the navy-yard near Portsmouth, New
Hampshire, it so happened that I was then stationed at that yard. Living in spacious quarters
as a bachelor, and not unwilling to share my
summer comforts with my friends, it occurred to
me that Hawthorne's interests could best be pro-
moted by bringing him and Mrs. Hawthorne into
social relations with some of my influential friends
and their wives.

To carry out this project, and for my personal
pleasure as well, I invited Senator and Mrs. Pierce
and Senator and Mrs. Atherton, of New Hampshire, and Senator Fairfield, of Maine, together
with Mr. and Mrs. Hawthorne and little Una, to
spend two or three weeks with me. To make
the reunion less formal, two of my own sisters
and some Washington friends were included.
The indulgent party enjoyed the novelty of a
visit to a bachelor at a navy-yard, and when any
shortcomings in his housekeeping occurred the
guests only grew the merrier therefor.

What with boating, fishing, and driving, and in
the entire absence of formality, the visit went off

smoothly, and its main object—that of interesting men of influence in Hawthorne's behalf—
was attained.

Though Pierce was an old friend, Atherton
and Fairfield first made the acquaintance of
Hawthorne at that time, and they became his
strong advocates and friends.

In June of the next year he was appointed
Surveyor.

———

Hawthorne's life flowed tranquilly for the next
three years, at the end of which period he was
removed by the Whig administration, under (in
that case, at least) the pernicious doctrine of ro-
tation in office.

With other friends I strove zealously to save
him, because he wished to retain the office. But
when the dismissal came I wrote my congratulations, telling him that he would now be obliged
to devote himself to his appropriate work in life.
Eight months after his official decapitation he
finished "The Scarlet Letter," and increased
fame, as well as freedom from pressing anxiety
about pecuniary matters, followed quickly upon
the publication of the great romance.

"SALEM, Feb. 4, 1850.

"DEAR BRIDGE,—I finished my book only yesterday, one end being in press in Boston, while the

CUSTOM-HOUSE, SALEM

HAWTHORNE'S BIRTHPLACE

other was in my head here in Salem; so that, as
you see, the story is at least fourteen miles long.

"I should make you a thousand apologies for
being so negligent a correspondent if you did
not know me of old, and, as you have tolerated
me so many years, I do not fear that you will
give me up now. The fact is, I have a natural
abhorrence of pen and ink, and nothing short of
absolute necessity ever drives me to them.

"My book, the publisher tells me, will not be
out before April. He speaks of it in tremendous
terms of approbation. So does Mrs. Hawthorne,
to whom I read the conclusion last night. It
broke her heart, and sent her to bed with a griev-
ous headache, which I look upon as a triumphant
success.

"Judging from its effect on her and the publisher, I may calculate on what bowlers call a
ten-strike. Yet I do not make any such calcu-
lation. Some portions of the book are power-
fully written; but my writings do not, nor ever
will, appeal to the broadest class of sympathies,
and therefore will not obtain a very wide popularity. Some like them very much, others care
nothing for them, and see nothing in them.
There is an introduction to this book giving a
sketch of my custom-house life, with an imagina-
tive touch here and there, which may, perhaps,
be more widely attractive than the main narra-

tive. The latter lacks sunshine, etc. To tell you
the truth, it is—(I hope Mrs. Bridge is not present)—it is positively a h—l-f—d story, into which
I found it almost impossible to throw any cheering light.

"'This house on Goose Creek, which you tell
me of, looks really attractive; but I am afraid
there must be a flaw somewhere. I like the rent
amazingly. I wish you would look at it and form
your own judgment and report accordingly; and,
should you decide favorably, I will come myself
and see it; but if it appears ineligible to you I
shall let the matter rest there, it being inconve-
nient for me to leave home, partly because funds
are to be husbanded at this juncture of my affairs, and partly because I can ill spare the time,
as winter is the season when my brain-work is
chiefly accomplished.

"I should like to give up the house which I now
occupy at the beginning of April, and must soon
make a decision as to where I shall go. I long
to get into the country, for my health latterly is
not quite what it has been for many years past.
I should not long stand such a life of bodily in-
activity and mental exertion as I have lived for
the last few months. An hour or two of daily
labor in a garden, and a daily ramble in country
air, or on the sea-shore, would keep all right.
Here, I hardly go out once a week. Do not al-

lude to this matter in your letters to me, as my wife already sermonizes me quite sufficiently on my habits; and I never own up to not feeling perfectly well. Neither do I feel anywise ill; but only a lack of physical vigor and energy, which reacts upon the mind.

"With our best regards to Mrs. Bridge, I remain, Truly your friend,

"NATH HAWTHORNE.

"HORATIO BRIDGE, Esq., U. S. Navy Yard, Portsmouth, N. H."

"SALEM, April 13, 1850.

"DEAR BRIDGE,—I am glad you like 'The Scarlet Letter.' It would have been a sad matter indeed if I had missed the favorable award of my oldest and friendliest critic. The other day I met with your notice of 'Twice-Told-Tales' for the Augusta *Age;* and I really think nothing better has been said about them since. This book has been highly successful: the first edition having been exhausted in ten days, and the second (five thousand copies in all) promising to go off rapidly.

"As to the Salem people, I really thought that I had been exceedingly good-natured in my treatment of them. They certainly do not deserve good usage at my hands after permitting me to be deliberately lied down—not merely once, but

8

at two several attacks—on two false indictments
—without hardly a voice being raised on my behalf; and then sending one of the false witnesses
to Congress, others to the Legislature, and choos-
ing another as the mayor.

" I feel an infinite contempt for them—and probably have expressed more of it than I intended—
for my preliminary chapter has caused the greatest uproar that has happened here since witch-
times. If I escape from town without being
tarred and feathered, I shall consider it good-
luck. I wish they would tar and feather me; it
would be such an entirely novel kind of distinction for a literary man. And, from such judges
as my fellow-citizens, I should look upon it as a
higher honor than a laurel crown.

" I have taken a cottage in Lenox, and mean to
take up my residence there about the first of
May. In the interim my wife and children are
going to stay in Boston; and nothing could be
more agreeable to myself than to spend a week
or so with you; so that your invitation comes exceedingly apropos. In fact, I was on the point
of writing to propose a visit. We shall move
our household gods from this locality to-morrow
or next day. I will leave my family at Dr. Peabody's, and come to Portsmouth on Friday of
this week, unless prevented from coming at all.
I shall take the train that leaves Boston at eleven

o'clock; so, if you happen to be in Portsmouth that afternoon, please to look after me. I am glad of this opportunity of seeing you, for I am assured you will never find your way to Lenox. I thank Mrs. Bridge for her good-wishes as respects my future removal from office, but I should be sorry to anticipate such bad-fortune as being ever again appointed to one.

"Truly your friend,

"NATH HAWTHORNE."

Hawthorne's feelings towards Salem and its inhabitants, as shown in the above letter, may be accounted for somewhat by the circumstances and surroundings of his boyhood.

The isolation of his family, his three years' lameness, and his long absences—at Raymond and in college—prevented him from forming friendships with other Salem boys that might have essentially modified his later sentiments towards his native town. As it was, he grew up almost as a stranger in his birthplace—until he had reached manhood. But I have seen no evidence of unfriendliness towards his fellow-citizens previous to his being brought into closer relations with them as an officer of the Salem Custom-house, from which office he was removed through the strenuous exertions of leading men of the opposite political party. As Hawthorne

had never been an active partisan, and as no
fault could justly have been found with his official or personal character, it was not strange that
he became embittered against many of the men
of influence in Salem and against the town itself.
And he did not attempt to conceal his sentiments, or to mollify the anger resulting from his
cutting statements in that regard !

CHAPTER XII

My own marriage in 1846 brought to Hawthorne another appreciative friend, to whom he
at once gave his confidence and esteem.

Our house was always open to him, and he
came to us at will, as to friends from whom he
was sure of a welcome and in whose society he
felt no restraint.

On one occasion, after my return from an African and European cruise, I was ordered to the
Portsmouth station, where we were hardly settled
at house-keeping when Hawthorne came to see us.

The hall was encumbered by boxes, at sight of
which he feared that his visit was inopportune;
and he quickly said, "I have just come for an
hour or two to see you, and must return this
evening."

Mrs. Bridge — perceiving that the fear of in-
commoding us was influencing him—said,

"Must you desert us when I need your aid in
unpacking these boxes?"

"Will you really let me help you?" he replied.

Her joking answer—assuring him of her pleasure in gaining so strong a helper, both in muscle and intelligence—put him entirely at ease, and for a week he made himself useful on all possible occasions. As I was convalescing, after a malarial fever, it was a great relief to me to have his efficient aid.

A pleasant feature of the work consisted in unpacking and selecting places for the many things that Mrs. Bridge had been able to collect in France and Italy during the troublous times of 1848–49.

Hawthorne was much interested in her account of the persons she had met and the places she had visited, but more especially of her journey in Spain.

Mrs. Bridge had come to join me in Europe; but, as I was attached to a cruising ship, we could only meet occasionally, and she was obliged to make her journeys without me.

At another time, on one of his visits, he was talking with Mrs. Bridge at twilight, while I was dozing on the sofa. With the ease of manner that precluded all embarrassment on his part, she said to him, "Now tell me a story." Looking at me—without a moment's hesitation—he said, "I will tell you one which I could write, making that gentleman one of the principal characters. I should begin with the description of his father—a dignified and conservative man —who, for many years, had lived in a great mansion, by the side of a noble river, and had daily enjoyed the sight of the beautiful stream flowing placidly by, without a thought of disturbing its natural course.

" His children had played upon its banks, and the boys swam in the quiet stream or rowed their boats thereon.

" But, after their father's decease, his sons, grown to manhood—progressive in unison with the spirit of the age—conceived the project of utilizing the great body of water flowing idly by. So, calling in the aid of a famous engineer, they built a high and costly dam across the river, thus creating a great water-power sufficient for the use of many prospective mills and factories.

" The river—biding its time—quietly allowed the obstructions to be finished; and then it rose in its wrath and swept away the expensive structure and the buildings connected with it, and took its course majestically to the sea.

" Nor did this satisfy the offended river-gods; for they cut a new channel for the stream, and swallowed up the paternal mansion of the young men, and desolated its beautiful grounds, thus showing the superior power of Nature whenever it chooses to assert itself."

The year after the visit just described—being still languid and debilitated—I accepted Hawthorne's invitation to come and see him and his family at Lenox in the Berkshire hills, a region famed for the healthfulness of its climate, and as the home of the Sedgwicks, Fanny Kemble Butler, etc.

Fashion had not then invaded these lovely hills, and the comparatively small society was noted for its simple mode of living, for its intelligence, and its culture.

The Hawthornes occupied an old-fashioned cottage, painted deep red, and overlooking a charming lake.

There were a great many deficiencies in the arrangements of the quaint old house and grounds, for which I had a quick eye, and to the immediate remedying of which Hawthorne and I devoted our efforts. Mrs. Hawthorne looked on with amused approval (even when our performances were rather revolutionary), as she saw us engaging, with great glee, in improving matters generally. Boxes were turned into closets and bookshelves, and the cellar and hen-house were not neglected.

A letter I wrote my wife from Lenox gives my own impressions of the surroundings of the Hawthornes, and of our occupations during my very pleasant visit:

"LA MAISON ROUGE, July 18, 1850.

"CARA MIA,—I must explain the meaning of
the caption. Be it known, then, that Hawthorne
occupies a house painted red, like some old-fashioned farm-houses you have seen. It is owned
by Mr. Tappan, who lived in it awhile; but he
is now at High-Wood, the beautiful place of Mr.
Ward. The old farm-house is quite comfortable,
having sufficient room, and being furnished simply and in good taste. All the surroundings give
proof of the easy circumstances of the present
occupants.

"The view of the lake is lovely; I have seldom
seen one so beautiful.

"Mr. and Mrs. Hawthorne are most friendly,
and my visit seems to give them much satisfaction.

"Nor am I quite useless. I have planned various improvements in the house and grounds,
including some in the hennery, where the nests
and roosts are now arranged according to the
directions of the best authors upon that useful
subject. To-morrow we are going to make some
closets and book-shelves of the boxes in which
the furniture came. As I am not so strong as
before my fever, Hawthorne does the hard work,
such as lifting, sawing, etc., while I plan and ham-
mer. Oh, we are a model pair of working-men—
the Man of Genius and the Naval Officer!

"The children behave very well, and, certainly, are charming youngsters. Una acts like a little lady, and exhibits good temper and obedience; while Julian is a good-natured, laughing young giant.

"We intend to visit High-Wood at an early day, and thence shall drive to the village, if we can get Mr. Tappan's vehicle.

"19th. It has rained all the forenoon. Consequently we have been at work in cellar, hennery, and shed. In the reorganized hennery our labor has already been justified, for no less than three hens have shown their approval of it by each laying an egg in a new and scientific nest.

"I have selected two boxes for the children's closets, besides a large one for a wardrobe, and another for a general closet; and, having laid out several days' work for somebody in papering, etc., I am satisfied.

"We have cleared up the wood-house and cellar, mended some chairs, and have done a great deal towards making the establishment 'shipshape' and comfortable.

"You must not think that I am exerting myself too much. Hawthorne has taken the hardest part of the work, and I really feel all the better for the exercise. . . .

"Hawthorne and his wife both send kindest regards. Ever yours, H."

As the "House of the Seven Gables" was at
that time in course of preparation, it is fair to
presume that the fowls, flowers, and vegetables
of the Red-house establishment were studies for
the pictures of Phœbe's garden favorites.

Hawthorne's residence at Lenox was marked
not only by the production of the "House of the
Seven Gables," but by that of the "Wonder-Book
for Girls and Boys," a volume of three hundred
pages, which he wrote in seven weeks, his facility for labor increasing with the public demand
for his writings. He also prepared, at that place,
a second volume of "Twice-Told-Tales" and began the "Blithedale Romance."

A few days after leaving Lenox I received the
following letter, which has in it an amusing touch
about the effect my active reforms had produced
upon the children.

"LENOX, Aug. 7, 1850.

"... Duyckink, of the *Literary World*, and
Herman Melville are in Berkshire, and I expect
them to call here this morning. I met Melville
the other day, and liked him so much that I have
asked him to spend a few days with me before
leaving these parts.

"We all have very pleasant recollections of
your visit. Julian broke a china cup a few days
ago, and very coolly remarked that "Mr. Bridge
could mend it.""

"We have got some maple-paper, and shall soon begin the transmutation of your boxes.

"We are getting along very well. Una and Julian grow apace, and so do our chickens, of which we have two broods. There is one difficulty about these chickens, as well as about the old fowls. We have become so intimately acquainted with every individual of them, that it really seems like cannibalism to think of eating them. What is to be done?

"With our best regards to Mrs. Bridge,
            "Yours truly,
                "NATH HAWTHORNE."

            "LENOX, March 15, 1851.

"DEAR BRIDGE,—I am glad to hear from you at last, although I am sorry you have sunk into the depths of official idleness, and have effected nothing towards the new edition of the "Cruiser."

"You know not what fame you may be flinging away. However, all that shall be made up in a journal or history of your next voyage. But I do most heartily wish that you would cut the Navy, and trust to God and your own exertions for a good life at home. Even such a poor house and poor fare as mine, for instance, are better than sea-biscuit and a stateroom.

"The 'House of the Seven Gables,' in my opinion, is better than 'The Scarlet Letter'; but I should not wonder if I had refined upon the principal character a little too much for popular appreciation; nor if the romance of the book should be found somewhat at odds with the humble and familiar scenery in which I invest it. But I feel that portions of it are as good as anything I can hope to write, and the publisher speaks encouragingly of its success.

"How slowly I have made my way in life! How much is still to be done! How little worth—outwardly speaking—is all that I have achieved! The bubble reputation is as much a bubble in literature as in war, and I should not be one whit the happier if mine were world-wide and time-long than I was when nobody but yourself had faith in me.

"The only sensible ends of literature are, first, the pleasurable toil of writing; second, the gratification of one's family and friends; and, lastly, the solid cash.

"Remember me to Mrs. Bridge, and give her, likewise, my wife's remembrances. I shall take advantage of a visit to Dr. Peabody in June next to go to Boston, and hope to have a meeting with you before my return.

"The boxes, I must confess, are not all papered, but neither are they all unpapered; and my wife was talking of doing the remainder only the day before your letter arrived.

"Your friend,   N. H."

"LENOX, July 22, 1851.

"DEAR BRIDGE,—What a long, long while since I have heard from you! I don't know when it was, or which of us wrote last, though I am, most probably, in your debt for a letter; but a weary scribbler, like myself, must be allowed a great deal of license as regards debts of that nature. Why did you not write and tell me how you liked, or how you did not like, the 'House of the Seven Gables'? Did you feel shy of expressing an unfavorable opinion? It would not have hurt me in the least, though I am always glad to please you; but I rather think I have reached that stage when I do not care, very essentially one way or the other, for anybody's opinion on any one production. On this last romance, for instance, I have heard and seen such diversity of judgment that I should be altogether bewildered if I attempted to strike a balance. So I take nobody's estimate unless it happens to agree with my own. I think it a work more characteristic of my mind, and more proper and natural for me to write, than 'The Scarlet Letter'; but for that very reason, less likely to interest the public. Nevertheless it appears to have sold better than the former, and, I think, is more sure of retaining the ground it acquires. Mrs. Kemble writes that both works are popular in England, and advises me to take out my copyright there.

" Since the first of June I have written a book of two or three hundred pages for children ; and I think it stands a chance of a wide circulation. The title, at all events, is an *ad captandum* one— ' The Wonder-Book for Girls and Boys.' I don't know what I shall write next. Should it be a romance, I mean to put an extra touch of the devil into it, for I doubt whether the public will stand two quiet books in succession without my losing ground. As long as people will buy, I shall keep at work, and I find that my facility for labor increases with the demand for it.

" Mrs. Hawthorne published a little work two months ago, which still lies in sheets, but I assure you it makes some noise in the world, both by day and night. In plain English, we have another little daughter ; a very bright, strong, and healthy miss ; but at present with no pretensions to beauty. Sophia intends, in the course of two or three weeks, to take the baby to Mr. Mann's in West Newton, on a short visit. Una will accompany her, and I shall remain here with Julian. After her return I shall go to Boston, and, if you should be still at Portsmouth, I will run down thither to see you, if for no more than a day. It is now above a year since I have been ten miles from this place, and I begin to need a little change of scene.

"We intend to take Mrs. Kemble's house in October or the beginning of November. She offered it last year for nothing; but I declined the terms. She offers it now for the same rent that I pay here; and, though this is inadequate, yet as she cannot let the house on any other terms, or to any other person, I see no impropriety in my accepting the offer. If she could do better, I would not take it. We shall lose a beautiful prospect, and gain a much more convenient and comfortable house than our present one. If I continue to prosper in my literary vocation, I mean to buy a house before a great while, but it shall not be in Berkshire. I prefer the sea-coast, both as a matter of taste and because I think it suits both Sophia's constitution and my own better than this hill country.

"Do write and tell me of your welfare and prospects. I am afraid you will not be able to read this scrawl, but I have contracted a bad habit of careless penmanship.

"With our best regards to Mrs. Bridge,
    "Your friend,   NATH HAWTHORNE."

After receiving this letter, I wrote Hawthorne

of the old family home of the Sparhawks, at Kittery Point, which was then for sale, and was not far from the cottage near the sea which I had just bought.

"LENOX, Oct. 11. 1852.

"DEAR BRIDGE,—The Sparhawk house certainly offers some temptations, among which, however, I do not reckon that hideous story of the howling dead man, but I shall resist them. It is too much out of the way. I have learned pretty well the desirableness of an easy access to the world; and you will learn it, too, if you should ever actually occupy your island purchase. You will never be able to make that your permanent home. I am sure of it. It will do well enough to play Robinson Crusoe for a summer or so, but when a man is making his settled dispositions for life, he had better be on the mainland, and as near a railroad station as possible.

"My 'Wonder-Book,' I suppose, will be out soon. I do not know your direction in Boston, so cannot send you one unless first advised thereof; but will tell the publishers to hand you one when called for. I have also a new volume of 'Twice-Told-Tales' in press and a new romance in futurity.

"We shall leave here, with much joy, on the first day of December.

"With our best regards to Mrs. Bridge, whom

9

I would not have missed seeing, only it involved
the not seeing my wife the next day.

"Truly yours,   NATH HAWTHORNE."

In the year of grace 1890 the historic "Red
House" was burned, and now only the blackened
ruins near the lovely lake remain to mark the spot
where it had stood so long.   In that "little red
shanty," as Mrs. Hawthorne called it, Hawthorne
wrote the "House of the Seven Gables" and the
"Wonder-Book for Girls and Boys," and there he
began the "Blithedale Romance."   In that house,
too, Rose (now Mrs. Lathrop) was born. To that
little, low-studded, yet cheerful dwelling, for nearly forty years after the departure of the man who
made it famous, visitors, in yearly increasing
numbers, resorted as to a shrine of genius purely
American.   Mr. Tappan, owner of the place, had
the good taste as well as the kindly remembrances
which led him to keep the study in the same state
that Hawthorne left it in.

"CONCORD, Mass., Oct. 18, 1852.

"DEAR BRIDGE,—I received your letter some
time ago, and ought to have answered it long
since, but you know my habits of epistolary de-
linquency, so I make no apology. Besides, I
have been busy with literary labor of more kinds
than one.   Perhaps you have seen 'Blithedale'

before this time. I doubt whether you will like
it very well; but it has met with good success,
and has brought me—besides its American circulation — a thousand dollars from England;
whence, likewise, have come many favorable
notices. Just at this time I rather think your
friend stands foremost there as an American fiction-monger.

"In a day or two I intend to commence a new
romance, which, if possible, I mean to make more
genial than the last.

"I did not send you the 'Life of Pierce,' not
considering it fairly one of my literary productions.

"I was terribly reluctant to undertake this
work, and tried to persuade Pierce—both by letter and *viva voce*—that I could not perform it so
well as many others; but he thought differently;
and, of course, after a friendship of thirty years,
it was impossible to refuse my best efforts in his
behalf at this—the great pinch of his life.

"Other writers might have made larger claims
for him, and have eulogized him more highly;
but I doubt whether any other could have bestowed a better aspect of sincerity and reality on
the narrative, and have secured all the credit
possible for him without spoiling all by asserting
too much.

"Before undertaking it, I made an inward res-

olution that I would accept no office from him ;
but, to say the truth, I doubt whether it would
not be rather folly than heroism to adhere to this
purpose in case he should offer me anything particularly good. We shall see. A foreign mission
I could not afford to take. The consulship at
Liverpool I might. I have several invitations
from English celebrities to come over there, and
this office would make all straight. What luck
that fellow has ! I have wanted you here while
writing up his memoirs for the sake of talking
over his character with you, as I cannot with
any other person. I have come seriously to the
conclusion that he has in him many of the chief
elements of a great ruler. His talents are ad-
ministrative ; he has a subtle faculty of making
affairs roll onward according to his will, and of
influencing their course without showing any
trace of his action. There are scores of men in
the country that seem brighter than he is; but
Frank has the directing mind, and will move
them about like pawns on a chess-board, and
turn all their abilities to better purpose than they
themselves could do. Such is my idea of him
after many an hour of reflection on his character
while making the best of his biography. He is
deep, deep, deep. But what luck withal ! Nothing can ruin him.

" Nevertheless I do not feel very sanguine

about the result of this election. There is
hardly a spark of enthusiasm in either party;
but what there is, so far as I can judge, is on the
side of Scott. The prospect is none of the brightest, either in New York, Ohio, or Pennsylvania;
and unless Frank gets one of them, he goes to
the wall. He himself does not appear to admit
the possibility of failure; but I doubt whether, in
a position like his, a man can ever form a reliable judgment of the prospect before him.

"Should he fail, what an extinction it will be!
He is in the intensest blaze of celebrity. His portrait is everywhere—in all the shop-windows, and
in all sorts of styles—on wood, steel, and copper;
on horseback, on foot, in uniform, in citizen's
dress, in iron medallions, in little brass medals,
and on handkerchiefs; and it seems as if the
world were full of his not very striking physiognomy.

"If he loses the election, in one little month
he will fall utterly out of sight and never come
up again. He is playing a terrible game, and for
a tremendous stake. On one side power, the
broadest popularity, and a place in history; on
the other (for I doubt whether it would not prove
a knock-down blow) oblivion, or death and a forgotten grave. He says, however, that he should
bear defeat with equanimity. Perhaps he might,
but I think he is not aware of the intense excite-

ment in which he lives. He seems calm, but his hair is whitening, I assure you. Well, three weeks more will tell the story.

"By the by, he speaks most kindly of you, and his heart seems to warm towards all his old friends under the influence of his splendid prospects. If he wins he will undoubtedly seek for some method of making you the better for his success. I love him, and, oddly enough, there is a kind of pitying sentiment mixed up with my affection for him just now.

"Yours truly,

"NATH HAWTHORNE."

CHAPTER XIII.

IMMEDIATELY after General Pierce's election to the Presidency, in 1852, he offered Hawthorne the Liverpool consulate, an office then considered the most lucrative of all the foreign appointments in the Presidential gift, and soon after his inauguration he gave him that place.

With his family, Hawthorne sailed for England in July, 1853.

His European life has been fully described by other writers; yet it may be well to give here a few of his letters from abroad, which speak of his annoyances at the prospect, and subsequent realization, of the decrease of his official emoluments by legislation, of his solicitude for the welfare of our country, and of some other matters of public or private concern.

"LIVERPOOL, March 30, 1854.

"MY DEAR BRIDGE,—You are welcome home, and I heartily wish I could see Mrs. Bridge and yourself and little Marian by our English fireside.

"I like my office well enough, but any official

duties and obligations are irksome to me beyond
expression. Nevertheless, the emoluments will be
a sufficient inducement to keep me here, though
they are not above a quarter part what some people suppose them.

" It sickens me to look back to America. I am
sick to death of the continual fuss and tumult
and excitement and bad blood which we keep up
about political topics. If it were not for my children I should probably never return, but—after
quitting office—should go to Italy, and live and
die there. If Mrs. Bridge and you would go, too,
we might form a little colony amongst ourselves,
and see our children grow up together. But it
will never do to deprive them of their native
land, which I hope will be a more comfortable
and happy residence in their day than it has
been in ours. In my opinion, we are the most
miserable people on earth.

" I wish you would send me the most minute
particulars about Pierce—how he looks and be-
haves when you meet him, how his health and
spirits are—and above all, what the public really
thinks of him—a point which I am utterly unable
to get at through the newspapers. Give him my
best regards, and ask him whether he finds his
post any more comfortable than I prophesied it
would be.

" I have a great deal more to say, but defer it

to future letters.   Mrs. Hawthorne sends her love
to Mrs. Bridge.   She is not very well, being unfavorably affected by this wretched climate.   The
children flourish, and will, I think, be permanently benefited by their residence here.

"Write me often, for I have now learned to
know how valuable a friend's letters are in a foreign land.

"Most truly yours,

"NATH HAWTHORNE."

U. S. CONSULATE, LIVERPOOL, April 17, 1854.

"DEAR BRIDGE,—I trust you received my letter, written a fortnight or thereabouts ago.

"As you are now in Washington, and, of course,
in frequent communication with Pierce, I want
you to have a talk with him on my affairs.   O'Sullivan, who arrived here a day or two ago, tells me
that a bill is to be brought forward in relation to
diplomatic and consular offices, and that, by
some of its provisions, a salary is to be given to
certain of the consulates.   I trust, in Heaven's
mercy, that no change will be made as regards the
emoluments of the Liverpool consulate—unless
indeed a salary is to be given in addition to the
fees; in which case I should receive it very thank-
fully.   This, however, is not to be expected; and
if Liverpool is touched at all, it will be to limit
its emoluments by a fixed salary—which will ren-

der the office not worth any man's holding. It
is impossible (especially for a man with a family
and keeping any kind of an establishment) not
to spend a vast deal of money here. The office,
unfortunately, is regarded as one of great dignity, and puts the holder on a level with the highest society, and compels him to associate on
equal terms with men who spend more than my
whole income on the mere entertainments and
other trimmings and embroidery of their lives.
Then I feel bound to exercise some hospitality
towards my own countrymen. I keep out of society as much as I decently can, and really prac-
tise as stern an economy as ever I did in my life;
but, nevertheless, I have spent many thousands
of dollars in the few months of my residence
here, and cannot reasonably hope to spend less
than six thousand per annum, even after all the
expenditure of setting up an establishment is defrayed. All this is for the mere indispensable
part of my living, and unless I make a hermit of
myself, and deprive my wife and children of all
the pleasures and advantages of our English residence, I must inevitably exceed the sum named
above. Every article of living has nearly doubled
in cost within a year. It would be the easiest
thing in the world for me to run in debt, even
taking my income at $15,000 (out of which all
the clerks, etc., are to be paid), the largest sum

that it ever reached in Crittenden's time. He had no family but a wife, and lived constantly at a boarding-house, and nevertheless went home, as he assured me, with an aggregate of only $25,000, derived from his official savings.

" Now the American public can never be made to understand such a statement as the above, and they would grumble awfully if more than six thousand per annum were allowed for a consul's salary ; yet it would not be worth my keeping at ten thousand dollars. I beg and pray, therefore, that Pierce will look at the reason and common sense of this business, and not let Mr. Dudley Mann shave off so much as a half-penny from my official emoluments. Neither do I believe that we have a single consulship in any part of the world, the net emoluments of which overpay the trouble and responsibility of the office. If these are lessened, the incumbent must be compelled to turn his official position to account by engaging in commerce—a course which ought not to be permitted, and which no Liverpool consul has ever adopted.

" After all, it is very possible that no change is contemplated as regards the large consulships. If so, I beg Mr. Dudley Mann's pardon.

" Tell the President that I was a guest at a public entertainment the other day, where his health was drunk standing, immediately after

those of the Queen and the Royal family. When
the rest of the party sat down, I remained on my
legs and returned thanks in a very pretty speech,
which was received with more cheering and ap-
plause than any other during the dinner. I think
it was altogether the most successful of my ora-
torical efforts — of which I have made several
since arriving here.

"I wish you would get some of your Congres-
sional friends to send me whatever statistical
documents are published by Congress, and also
any others calculated to be of use. I am daily
called upon for information respecting America,
which I do not always possess the materials to
give in a reliable shape.

"Your friend in haste,

"NATH HAWTHORNE."

April 18, 1854.

"DEAR BRIDGE,—

    *   *   *   *   *

"To drop the subject of my official emoluments and take up your own affairs, I must say,
after due thought, I feel somewhat desirous that
you should remain at Washington, not on your own
account, but on Pierce's. I feel a sorrowful sympathy for the poor fellow (for God's sake don't
show him this), and hate to have him left without one true friend, or one man who will speak

a single word of truth to him. There is no truer
man in the world than yourself, and unless you
have let him see a coolness on your part, he will
feel the utmost satisfaction in having you near
him. You will soon find, if I mistake not, that
you can exercise a pretty important influence
over his mind ; and such is my confidence in
your good judgment, and perfect faith in your
honesty, that I doubt not your influence would
be for his good. Of course it requires a good
deal of tact to fill such an office as I suggest, but
upon my honor, so far as actual power goes, I
would as lief have it as that of Secretary of State.
At all events, if you did nothing else, you might
do his heart good. . . . Regards to Mrs. Bridge.

"Truly yours,

"NATH HAWTHORNE."

U. S. CONSULATE, LIVERPOOL, Dec. 8, 1854.

"DEAR BRIDGE,—I send the leaves from an
almanac showing the British consular salaries, as
mentioned in my last. Of course these are in
addition to the official fees, which are mainly
similar to our own.

"Do you know Captain G——, the claimant
on the Dutch Government? I endorsed a draft
of £30 for him in order to enable him to take
passage by one of the Cunard steamers ; and he
writes me that he has been unable to provide for

its payment. I have directed Ticknor to pay the
draft, and have requested G—— to hand the
amount to you as soon as he may be able—which,
I fear, will not be in a hurry. He is a good fellow
and of honorable intentions, but seems to be involved in great difficulties. He is at present in or
about Washington. I do not wish you to suggest
to him the payment of the £30; but only to stand
ready to receive the money should he offer it. I
do not doubt his honorable purposes, but very
much doubt his ability.

" I should really be ashamed to tell you how
much my income is taxed by the assistance which
I find it absolutely necessary to render to American citizens who come to me in difficulty or dis-
tress. Every day there is some new claimant for
whom the Government makes no provision, and
whom the consul must assist, if at all, out of his
own pocket.

" It is impossible (or at any rate very disagreeable) to leave a countryman to starve in the
streets, or to hand him over to the charities of
an English work-house; so I do my best for these
poor devils. But I doubt whether they will meet
with quite so good treatment after the passage of
the Consular bill. If the Government chooses to
starve the consul, a good many will starve with
him.   Your friend,   N. H."

" U. S. Consulate, Liverpool, Dec. 14, 1854.

" Dear Bridge,—The real and substantial ar-
gument against the passage of the Consular bill
is, that it is an ill-considered and badly contrived
one.   It was drawn up, I presume, by Mr. Dudley Mann, whom—from what little I know of his
doings—I do not greatly respect as a public officer.   Just think of a man sitting in his office at
Washington and arranging salaries all over the
world, of his own mere motion ; without a single
inquiry into the peculiar circumstances, the expenses, the labor, etc., attending the different
positions ! At many consulates to which he as-
signs a less sum than to mine, there would be a
much greater balance accruing to the consul on
account of his smaller expenditure in clerk-hire
and office-rent.   A thorough preliminary investigation should be made, and, after ascertaining
the necessities of each office, the whole might
be arranged in a manner similar to the custom-
houses and to every other department of public
business.   This would have the effect of making
the consular clerks the servants and subordinates
of the State Department instead of hangers-on of
the consul, as they now are.   Should the proposed bill pass, it cannot possibly stand for any
length of time, because it is really not on a right
principle ; but it would be very little comfort to
me to see it altered a year or two after I go out

of office. I apprehend that the necessity of making some addition to the emoluments of diplomatic officers may carry through these consular measures—both being included in one bill. If they could be separated there would be little hazard of the passage of a consular bill, during this session at least.

"Finally, if the bill must pass, I trust, in Heaven's mercy, that it will not take effect from the signature of the act, but from the beginning of the next fiscal year.

"I admire the English practice in these matters. When an office is suppressed, they pay a liberal compensation to the incumbent, or pension him off; and they never diminish the income of an office except prospectively—to take effect on the appointment of a new man.

"My best regards to your wife. I wish our children could know one another; but this does not seem very probable at present. Whether I resign the consulship or not, I am likely to spend a long time abroad; for I can live economically in Italy, and can pursue my literary avocations as well there as elsewhere.

"Your friend,
                         "NATH HAWTHORNE."

"P.S.—Write me about Pierce, and how his health and spirits are. I ought to write to him, but it is a devilish sight harder to write to the

President of the United States (especially when he has been an intimate friend) than to a private man. It is my instinct to turn the cold shoulder on persons in his position."

"U. S. Consulate, Liverpool, March 23, 1855.

"Dear Bridge,—I thank you for all your efforts against this bill, but Providence is wiser than we are, and, doubtless, it will all turn out for the best.

"All through my life I have had occasion to observe that what seemed to be misfortunes have proved in the end to be the best things that could possibly have happened to me; and so it will be with this—even though the mode in which it benefits me should never be made clear to my apprehension. It would seem to be a desirable thing enough that I should have had a sufficient income to live comfortably upon for the rest of my life, without the necessity of labor; but, on the other hand, I might have sunk prematurely into intellectual sluggishness—which now there will be no danger of my doing; though, with a house and land of my own, and a good little sum at interest beside, I need not be under very great anxiety for the future. When I contrast my present situation with what it was five years ago, I see a vast deal to be thankful for; and I still hope to thrive by my legitimate instrument—the pen.

10

"One consideration, which goes very far towards reconciling me to quitting the office, is my wife's health, with which the English climate does not agree, and which I hope will be greatly benefited by a winter in Italy. In short, we have wholly ceased to regret the action of Congress (which nevertheless was most unjust and absurd), and are looking at matters on the bright side.

*   *   *   *   *

"I don't see how the next consul is to get along here, unless he be either a rich man or a rogue. God knows he will find temptations enough to be the latter.

"Give our best regards to Mrs. Bridge. How I wish you could spend the next two years with us in Italy.   Truly your friend,

"NATH HAWTHORNE."

"LIVERPOOL, April 13, 1855.

*   *   *   *   *

"We are in good spirits—my wife and I—about official emoluments. I shall have about as much money as will be good for me. Enough to educate Julian, and portion off the girls in a moderate way, that is, reckoning my pen as good for something. And, if I die, or am brain-stricken, my family will not be beggars, the dread of which has often troubled me in times past.

"I pray Heaven that your little girl is doing

HORATIO BRIDGE

well. We have been rather alarmed about her ever since you wrote that she had a congestion of the lungs, at least my wife has, and she alarmed me. But we hope and pray for the best.

"With our kindest regards to Mrs. Bridge,

"Your friend,   N. H."

"LIVERPOOL., April 26, 1855.

"MY DEAR BRIDGE,—May God support you and your wife in this great affliction. I hardly feel as if so old a friend as myself could venture a word of consolation; but, some time or other, I trust you will be able to feel that, though it is good to have a dear child on earth, it is likewise good to have one safe in Heaven. She will await you there, and it will seem like home to you now. My wife joins with me in the deepest sympathy for you and yours.

"Most affectionately,

"NATH HAWTHORNE."

The health of Mrs. Hawthorne, always delicate, being unfavorably affected by the English climate, the President, in 1855, considerately thought it might be beneficial to her, as well as gratifying to her husband, if he were transferred to a post where the climate was milder, and where Hawthorne himself would hold a diplomatic instead of a consular position.

As I was then stationed in Washington, the, President authorized me to offer, in a private letter to Hawthorne, the appointment of Chargéd'Affaires at Lisbon.

The subjoined letters show the considerations that governed the decision arrived at.

"U. S. CONSULATE, LIVERPOOL, August 24, 1855.

"MY DEAR BRIDGE,—I do not find it easy to come to any conclusion as respects the matter broached in your last. Many objections occur to me; for instance, my unacquaintance with diplomacy, and my dislike of the forms and ceremonies amid which diplomatists spend their time; also that I do not understand the Portuguese lingo, and have not any practice in French as a spoken language. Furthermore, it is a question whether Pierce can show me any further favors without exciting the remark that he is doing too much for a private friend. It is also a question with me whether I can afford to take the office, it being still, according to Cushing's opinion, a mere chargé-ship with only $4500 salary; and such it must remain for some months to come. I am inclined to think, therefore, that I had better hold on for another year to my consulship, and suffer the forfeiture of salary during my absence on the Continent, since it cannot be helped. I should not wish to keep the Portuguese mission more than a year, and I think it would not pay its expenses for that time. But it was a most kind and generous thing in the President to entertain the idea of transferring me thither, and you must express to him my sense of his kindness. My stay on the Continent will not probably be very long. I shall merely establish Mrs. Hawthorne there, and return.

"On the other hand, it will be so delightful to carry her to a delicious climate, and to remain there with her, that I feel no small hesitation in absolutely deciding to refuse the Portuguese place, should it be offered me. I hope Pierce will not offer it, for I cannot answer for myself that I shall do what really seems to me the wisest thing—that is, refuse it.

"You will observe that the higher rank and position of a minister, as compared with a consul, have no weight with me. This is not the kind of honor of which I am ambitious.

"With best regards to Mrs. Bridge,
     "Your friend,
          "NATH HAWTHORNE."

"U. S. CONSULATE, LIVERPOOL, August 31, 1855.

"DEAR BRIDGE,—I wrote you per last steamer, in reference to what you suggested about the Lisbon mission. My ideas have not changed as respects the inexpediency of my taking that post,

should it be offered me.   I shall act more wisely
to remain here, where I have gained some facility
in transacting the business ; and (unless Congress
interferes unfavorably with the present arrangement) I think this consulate will be as good as
the Lisbon mission, in a pecuniary way.

"But, though I conclude not to go thither myself, I am going to send Mrs. Hawthorne to Lisbon
in my stead.   The O'Sullivans have earnestly
invited her to come; and as they spent a considerable time with us in England, she is on the
most affectionate terms with them, and has con-
sented to go.   This relieves me of a very great
care and anxiety.   It is not improbable that I
shall wish to pay her a short visit before spring,
but I might go and come in a fortnight or three
weeks. Julian remains with me in England. Mrs.
Hawthorne and the other two children will probably sail in the course of a month.   If O'Sullivan
goes to Vienna he can convoy my wife to Malta,
or to any part of Italy.   Her health is better than
it was, but I think it best to be on the safe side
by sending her out of England.

"I made a blunder in my last letter to you.   A
new appointment to Lisbon would, at once, enable
me to receive the increased salary of $7500.   I
don't want it, however.

> "Truly yours,
>   "NATH HAWTHORNE."

"LIVERPOOL, June 6, 1856.

"DEAR BRIDGE,—

* * * * *

"You will see by the newspapers that John Bull
is in a pretty high state of excitement in relation
to American affairs; but, in my opinion, Frank
Pierce has taken the right course to bring matters to an amicable settlement. The recognition
of Walker was a prudent measure as well as a
decided one. It has angered the British, and
has mortified them to the heart's core; but it
has satisfied them that we are in earnest, and
that their further action will be in peril of a war,
which they would be very loath to encounter.
They show unmistakable tokens of backing out.
I should have been glad if intelligence of Graf-
ton's dismissal had accompanied that of the recognition, for it seems impossible that our Government can mean to retain him there, and any
delay only serves to keep the sore open.

"I am expecting Mrs. Hawthorne back from
Madeira in about ten days. The last accounts
of her health have been encouraging, but I see
little reason to think that she will be able to
encounter another English winter. Unless she
proves to be perfectly cured of her cough, I shall
make arrangements to give up the consulate in
the latter part of autumn, and we will be off for
Italy. I wish I were a little richer; but when I

compare my situation with what it was before the publication of the 'Scarlet Letter,' I have reason to be satisfied with my run of luck. And, to say the truth, I had rather not be *too* prosperous. It may be superstition, but it seems to me that the bitter is very apt to come with the sweet; and bright sunshine casts a dark shadow. So I content myself with a moderate portion of sugar, and about as much sunshine as that of an English summer's day. In this view of the matter I am disposed to thank God for the gloom and chill of my early life, in the hope that my share of adversity came then, when I bore it alone, and therefore it need not come now, when the cloud would involve those whom I love.

"I make my plans to return to America in about two years from this time. For my own part, I should be willing to stay abroad much longer, and perhaps even to settle permanently in Italy; but the children must not be kept away so long as to lose their American characteristics, otherwise they would be exiles and outcasts through life.

"Give my most sincere regards to Mrs. Bridge. I shall have few pleasanter anticipations when I return to America than that of seeing you both.

"Your friend,
"NATH HAWTHORNE."

"LIVERPOOL, June 20, 1856.

* * * * *

"You pain me by your gloomy view of political affairs, but I have great hope and faith that all will turn out well. As regards our relations with England, the course of our Government deserves all praise, and the result is a triumph that will be felt and recognized long hereafter. Frank has brought us safely and honorably through a great crisis; and England begins now to understand her own position and ours, and will never again assume the tone which hitherto she has always held towards us.

"Mrs. Hawthorne arrived at Southampton about a fortnight since, in much better health than I expected to see her, with little or no cough, or other disorder of any kind. She thinks, with great certainty, that she can safely spend another winter in England, and, if so, I shall not resign until the next Administration comes in. She is now staying at a country-house near Southampton, but I shall establish her in the neighborhood of London in the beginning of July.

"I am sorry Frank has not the nomination if he wished it. Otherwise I am glad he is out of the scrape.

"With best regards to Mrs. Bridge,
   "Your friend,
     "NATH HAWTHORNE."

" DEAR BRIDGE,—Your being located at Washington may, perhaps, enable you to assist me in
a matter which I wish to have suitably arranged.
I do not wish to retain the consulate for any
long period under the next Administration; and
I intend to leave England for the Continent
early in the ensuing autumn, unless Mr. Buchanan should take it into his head to remove me
(which I do not see why he should, as we are
personally friends, and there are no official
grounds against me). I shall resign, to take
effect on the thirty-first of August, at furthest;
and I wish the fact to be communicated to him
at the proper time, as he will doubtless be glad
to have the office at his disposal. If he wishes
for it sooner than the time above mentioned, he
will have to make the vacancy; and in view of
the possibility that he may choose to do so, I do
not like to do what, in effect, would be asking
for a few months of official tenure; but I author-
ize you to let my purpose be known in the proper quarter, and I shall consider myself bound in
honor to resign at the time stated. God knows I
am weary of the office, and would not have kept it
a great while longer under any circumstances.

" Mrs. Hawthorne and the children are now
residing in Southport, a little watering-place in
this vicinity, and I am happy to say that her

health is essentially improved.   A year or two in Italy will, with God's blessing, entirely set her up.

"Remember me kindly to Frank when you see him.   With my best regards to Mrs. Bridge,

"Truly yours,   NATH HAWTHORNE."

"LIVERPOOL, Jan. 15, 1857.

"DEAR BRIDGE,—Yours of the 23d ult. is received, and I have read it with much interest.   I regret that you think so doubtfully (or, rather, despairingly) of the prospects of the Union; for I should like well enough to hold on to the old thing.   And yet I must confess that I sympathize to a large extent with the Northern feeling, and think it is about time for us to make a stand.   If compelled to choose, I go for the North.   At present we have no country—at least, none in the sense an Englishman has a country.   I never conceived, in reality, what a true and warm love of country is till I witnessed it in the breasts of Englishmen.   The States are too various and too extended to form really one country.   New England is quite as large a lump of earth as my heart can really take in.

"Don't let Frank Pierce see the above, or he would turn me out of office, late in the day as it is.   However, I have no kindred with, nor leaning towards, the Abolitionists.

*   *   *   *   *

"To return to Frank Pierce, is it true that he thinks of returning into the Senate? I see nothing better to be done. He must have an occupation, and this would give him one, as well as dignified and useful position. And it would afford him an opportunity to explain himself to the country, and to win a better fame than he now retires with. But could he be elected?

"I wrote to you a short time since, communicating my purpose to resign at an early date, under Buchanan's Administration, and authorizing you to communicate the purpose to the President-elect. I think by next steamer (or very soon, at any rate) I had better write a formal letter of resignation, and send it to your care, to be delivered as soon as the new Administration comes in. My successor could then be nominated before the Senate adjourns, and, on many accounts, I should like to know who it will be. He will have a difficult post, and not a lucrative one, for my English clerks will retire with me, and he cannot supply their places with Americans at twice the expense. The new consul should be a hard-working man of business, for the emoluments of the office will no longer admit of his devolving its duties on subordinates. It is really a pity that such a comfortable berth should have been spoiled, but it has served my turn pretty well.

"Mrs. Hawthorne is tolerably well, and the children perfectly so. With kindest regards to Mrs. Bridge,

"Most truly yours,

"NATH HAWTHORNE."

"LIVERPOOL, Feb. 13, 1857.

"DEAR BRIDGE,—I enclose a letter to the President (viz. Buchanan, but I cannot address him as such by name until after the fourth of March) resigning my office, to take effect on and after the 31st of August next. This I wish you to deliver as soon as you think proper after the Inauguration. If he wants the office sooner, he is welcome to remove me ; but I should suppose, as it could not be done without some slight odium, that he would prefer my offered resignation.

"Mrs. Hawthorne and the children are all pretty well, and still continue at Southport. Mrs. H. and myself intend to travel about England and Scotland quite extensively between now and August, and we shall leave the children at Southport under the care of the governess until we all go to the Continent together.

"It will be a great relief to me to find myself a private citizen again; and I think the old literary instincts and habits will begin to revive in due season. I doubt, however, whether I pub-

lish a book until after my return to the United
States, which probably will not be in less than
two years.   I expect to live beyond my income
while on the Continent, but hope to bring myself
up again after my return with my literary labor,
and the economy of living on my own homestead.

*   *   *   *   *

" I wish you would see Pierce, and beg him,
from me, to say one word to Buchanan in reference to O'Sullivan.   He has spent more than
his income during all the time that he has been
at Lisbon, until since the commencement of the
present year.   If turned out now he is irremedi-
ably ruined.   He is (as Pierce well knows) a
most excellent Minister ; and I do entreat him,
by all the love I feel for him (Pierce, I mean), to
do O'Sullivan this kindness.

" My best regards to Mrs. Bridge.

" Your friend,

" NATH HAWTHORNE."

Early in the third year of Hawthorne's residence at Liverpool he became weary of his position, and contemplated resigning it.   He had
realized enough to live upon " with comfortable
economy"; his income from his literary work was
considerable and increasing; and he wished to
travel about England and Scotland, and to spend
some years upon the Continent before returning

to America. The consulate had become less
profitable, and, more than all, the climate of
England had proved injurious to Mrs. Hawthorne's health. This last and weightiest consideration was obviated for a time by an invitation from Mr. and Mrs. O'Sullivan to spend the
winter with them in Lisbon and Madeira. So
great benefit to Mrs. Hawthorne's health resulted
from the visit that the contemplated resignation
was deferred until after the election of President
Buchanan. At length Hawthorne determined
to resign, and he authorized me to inform the
President of his purpose, at the same time enclosing to me his resignation, which was duly
delivered.

In the September next ensuing, a new consul
was sent to relieve Hawthorne, and he gladly returned to the condition of a private citizen. He
had, at different times, held three offices under
the United States Government, viz., those of
Weigher and Gauger in the Boston Custom-
house, of Surveyor in the Salem Custom-house,
and, finally, of Consul at Liverpool. In all these
places he for the time subordinated his finer and
higher faculties to his matter-of-fact duties, and
applied his common-sense to the prosaic tasks
that those commercial offices imposed. In all
of them he performed his obligations faithfully,
and to the entire satisfaction of the Government

and of those persons with whom he had official intercourse. I received the following letter from Hawthorne after his successor had been appointed:

"LIVERPOOL, Sept. 17, 1857.

"DEAR BRIDGE,—I have received your letter and the not unwelcome intelligence that there is another Liverpool consul now in existence. It is a pity you did not tell me how soon he will be here, for that is a point which must have a good deal of influence on my own movements. I am going to set out for Paris in a day or two with my wife and children, and shall leave them there while I return to await my successor. Poor fellow! being such as you describe him, he will soon find the resources of the consulate too narrow for him.

*   *   *   *   *

"I expect great pleasure and improvement during my stay on the Continent, and shall come home at last somewhat reluctantly. Your pledge in my behalf of a book shall be honored in due time if God pleases; but I doubt much whether I do anything more than observe and journalize while I remain abroad. It would be a crowning pleasure to Mrs. Hawthorne and me if Mrs. Bridge and you could join us in Italy. It is within the bounds of possibility that we may yet meet there.

" Mrs. H. and the children are now a hundred miles off, at Leamington, in the centre of England, or she would cordially join me in regards and remembrances to yourself and wife.

" Your friend,
" NATH HAWTHORNE."

— ——

In the story of Hawthorne's life in England, there is nothing more characteristic, nothing more noble, than his care for those Americans who came to him for advice or aid. Besides numerous instances of generosity never heard of by the public, there was a notable one in the case of Miss Delia Bacon, casually mentioned in " Our Old Home," under the head of " Recollections of a Gifted Woman."

Without assuming any credit for his action in the case, or even mentioning his disinterested aid to one who had no other claim upon him than that she was a lonely and friendless country-woman, he describes her patient labor in pursuit of what she devoutly believed to be the true secret of Shakespeare's identity.

Whether her theories were wholly visionary or not, she had the courage of her convictions, opposed as they were to the settled belief of the rest of the world, and she lived and died a martyr to the truth of history, as she regarded it.

11

When this singular woman had exhausted all her financial means, when her family and friends declined to assist her unless she would give up her chimerical pursuit and return to America, she — almost despairingly — appealed to Hawthorne; and he responded in a manner that displayed his nobleness of heart, by the way in which he aided the forlorn enthusiast in her direst need. It gives one a higher estimate of human nature to hear of such unselfishness, such unwearied patience, and such rare delicacy as were exhibited by Hawthorne in extending the moral and material aid which she was too proud to solicit.

The interesting " Life of Delia Bacon," by Theodore Bacon, published in 1888, contains some twenty letters of Hawthorne—therein for the first time made public—which charmingly display, in the words of Mr. Bacon, " the noble generosity, the unwearying patience, the exquisite considerateness with which for two years he (Hawthorne) gave unstinted help, even of that material sort which she would not ask for, to this lonely countrywoman."

In a postscript to one of these letters to Miss Bacon, Hawthorne writes, in almost apologetic terms: " You say nothing about the state of your funds. Pardon me for alluding to the subject, but you promised to apply to me in case of need. I am ready." Could an offer of assistance be more delicately expressed?

If there were no other proof of Hawthorne's appreciative regard for the friendless, it shines forth brightly in these private letters.

CHAPTER XIV.

In 1860, Hawthorne and his family returned to America after a seven years' absence, and went at once to "The Wayside," his Concord home, where he resided until his decease.

The following letter shows his deep thankfulness for the preservation of the lives of Mrs. Hawthorne and the children during their long absence abroad:

"CONCORD, MASS., July 3, 1860.

"DEAR BRIDGE,—Your letter has just reached me; not unexpectedly, for I felt quite sure that I should soon hear from you.

"We came hither directly on landing from the steamer. I have not left Mrs. Hawthorne behind, nor any one else that belongs to me, for which I heartily thank God. It is a blessing which, at one time, I scarcely hoped for.

"My friends tell me that I am very little changed, but, of course, seven years have done their work. The most perceptible alteration is a moustache of Italian growth.

"If you will give me timely notice I shall come to

Boston to meet you. Give all our kindest regards
to Mrs. Bridge, and believe me your friend—as
thirty-five years ago.

"NATH HAWTHORNE."

Hawthorne, on his return from Europe, found
the nation embroiled in an angry controversy between the two great political parties of the day,
and he viewed with the utmost solicitude the pre-
monitory symptoms of civil war, apparent in the
press and in Congress.

Early in the year next following the war-cloud
burst, and the struggle continued for four years
of tremendous effort and sacrifice on the part of
those who strove to destroy the Union, as well as
of their opponents, who, happily, were able to pre-
serve it.

It is well known that Hawthorne was a Democrat in principle. He was, however, neither ex-
treme nor narrow in his views, nor did he ever
take an active part in political controversies.
His "Life of Pierce" was written from personal
friendship and the true spirit of comradeship.
Political preference had little controlling force
in the matter.

In regard to Hawthorne's politics, let me here
revert to our college days and to the Presidential
election of 1824, which was preceded by the usual

political excitements, into which boys, as well as men, entered zealously. The students showed their individual preferences as strongly as, and much more disinterestedly than, the average voter at the outside polls. At that time Pierce, Cilley, Hawthorne, and the writer were enthusiastic supporters of General Jackson.

In later years, when the doctrine of abolition was prominently brought forward, Hawthorne, like conservative men of all parties, was outspoken against it. He held that the Constitution was valid and binding upon all the States, and that no one who did not recognize a higher law could honestly interfere with the institutions of the Southern States, as guaranteed to them by the Constitution.

But when the South declared for disunion, and fired on the old flag at Fort Sumter, Hawthorne, as did most Northern Democrats, unhesitatingly took his stand with the North, and strongly espoused the cause of the Union.

Like many other loyal men, he almost despaired of success; but he wished to "fight to the death for the Northern slave States, and let the rest go." He had no sympathy with the South during the rebellion, but he rejoiced in every Union victory, and approved and applauded the granting of liberal military supplies, and the vigorous prosecution of the war. In short, he was a Democrat before the rebellion, a War Democrat after it broke out.

CHAPTER XV

My own duties as Paymaster-General in charge of a naval bureau at Washington were too arduous and engrossing to allow much time to be given to private matters either of interest or friendship, yet I was glad to have a month's visit from Hawthorne in March and April of 1862.

He went occasionally to Congress, to the White House, and to other places of interest in Washington. He visited some of the neighboring battle-fields in company with Mrs. Bridge and Dicey, the English writer, and he made an excursion to McClellan's headquarters, another to Harper's Ferry, and a steamer trip with me to Norfolk.

During his visit he met many distinguished men, and gained a much clearer view of the war than he had before. His clever article in the *Atlantic Monthly* in 1862, entitled "Chiefly About War Matters," embodied the results of his observations.

The letter next following speaks of the Wayside, which was just finished, and gives some of

Hawthorne's views in relation to the war, as do
the two letters immediately following it.

"CONCORD, May 26, 1861.

*   *   *   *   *

"I am about making the final disbursements
on account of my house, which, of course, has
cost me three times the sum calculated upon. I
suppose every man, in summing up the cost of a
house, feels considerably like a fool; but it is the
first time, and will be the last, that I make a fool
of myself in this particular way. At any rate, the
result is a pretty and convenient house enough,
no larger than was necessary for my family and
an occasional friend, and no finer than a modest
position in life demands. The worst of it is, I
must give up all thoughts of drifting about the
world any more, and try to make myself at home
in one dull spot.

"It is rather odd, with all my tendency to stick
in one place, I yet find great delight in frequent
change; so that, in this point of view, I had
better not have burdened myself with taking a
house upon my back. Such change of quarters
as makes up the life of you naval men might have
suited me.

"The war, strange to say, has had a beneficial
effect upon my spirits, which were flagging wo-
fully before it broke out. But it was delightful

to share in the heroic sentiment of the time,
and to feel that I had a country—a consciousness
which seemed to make me young again. One
thing, as regards this matter, I regret, and one I
am glad of. The regrettable thing is that I am
too old to shoulder a musket myself, and the joyful thing is that Julian is too young. He drills
constantly with a company of lads, and he means
to enlist as soon as he reaches the minimum age;
but I trust that we shall either be victorious or
vanquished before that time. Meantime (though
I approve of the war as much as any man), I
don't quite understand what we are fighting for,
or what definite result can be expected. If we
pummel the South ever so hard, they will love us
none the better for it; and even if we subjugate
them, our next step should be to cut them adrift.
If we are fighting for the annihilation of slavery,
to be sure, it may be a wise object, and offers a
tangible result, and the only one which is consistent with a future reunion between North and
South. A continuance of the war would soon
make this plain to us, and we should see the expediency of preparing our black brethren for future citizenship by allowing them to fight for their
own liberties and educating them through heroic
influences.

"Whatever happens next, I must say that I rejoice that the old Union is smashed. We never

were one people, and never really had a country since the Constitution was formed.

"I trust you mean to come and bring Mrs. Bridge to see us this summer. I shall like my house twice as well when you have looked at it. We are all well. Write again.

"Your friend,
"NATH HAWTHORNE."

"CONCORD, Oct. 12, 1861.

"DEAR BRIDGE,—

*   *   *   *   *

"I am glad you take such a hopeful view of our national prospects so far as regards the war; but my own opinion is that no nation ever came safe and sound through such a confounded difficulty as this of ours. For my part I don't hope, nor indeed wish, to see the Union restored as it was. Amputation seems to me much the better plan, and all we ought to fight for is the liberty of selecting the point where our diseased members shall be lop't off. I would fight to the death for the Northern Slave States and let the rest go.

"I fully expected that you would pay me at least a flying visit while at the North this summer, but I suppose your time was brief and filled up with more essential matters.

"I have not found it possible to occupy my mind with its usual trash and nonsense during these anxious times, but, as the autumn advances, I find myself sitting down to my desk and blotting successive sheets of paper, as of yore. Very likely I may have something ready for the public long before the public is ready to receive it.

" We are all very well, and, in spite of public troubles, have spent a quiet and happy summer. I am glad Mrs. Bridge has had a little respite from Washington life, and heartily wish you had been with her. But honest men are of too much value and too rare to be spared from their posts in these times.

" Do write again, and enlighten me so far as you may as to what is going on.

" Your friend, NATH HAWTHORNE."

" CONCORD, Feb. 14, 1862.

" DEAR BRIDGE,— Your proposition that I should pay a visit to Washington is very tempting, and I should accept it if it were not for several 'ifs'—neither of them, perhaps, a sufficient obstacle in itself, but, united, pretty difficult to overcome. For instance, I am not very well, being mentally and physically languid; but I suppose there is about an even chance that the trip and change of scene might supply the energy which I lack. Also, I am pretending to write a book; and though I am no wise diligent about it, still, each week finds me a little more advanced, and I am now at a point where I do not like to leave it entirely. Moreover, I ought not to spend money needlessly in these hard times, for it is my opinion that the book-trade, and everybody connected with it, is bound to fall to zero before the war and the subsequent embarrassments come to an end.

"I might go on multiplying 'ifs,' but the above are enough. Nevertheless, as I said, I am greatly tempted by your invitation, and it is not impossible that, in the course of a few weeks, I may write to ask you if it still holds good. Meanwhile I send you enclosed a respectable old gentleman, who my friends say is very like me, and may serve as my representative. If you will send me a similar one of yourself, I shall be truly obliged.

"Frank Pierce came here and spent a night, a week or two since, and we mingled our tears and condolences for the state of the country. Pierce is truly patriotic, and thinks there is nothing left for us but to fight it out, but I should be sorry to take his opinion implicitly as regards our chances in the future. He is bigoted to the Union, and sees nothing but ruin without it: whereas I (if we can only put the boundary far enough south) should not much regret an ultimate separation. A few weeks will decide how this is to be, for, unless a powerful Union feeling shall be developed by the military successes that seem to be setting in, we ought to turn our attention to the best mode of resolving ourselves into two nations.   It would be too great an absurdity to spend all our Northern strength for the next generation in holding on to a people who insist on being let loose.   If we do hold them, I should think Sumner's territorial plan the best way.

"I trust your health has not suffered by the immense occupation which the war must have brought upon you. The country was fortunate in having a man like yourself in so responsible a situation—'faithful found among the faithless.'

"I wish I could hear from you oftener.   Shall you come to New England next summer?   If so do try (with Mrs. Bridge) to pay us a visit—the longer the better.

"My wife and family are quite well, and send their kindest regards to Mrs. Bridge and yourself.   Your friend,

"NATH HAWTHORNE.

"P.S.—I ought to thank you for a shaded map of negrodom,* which you sent me a little while ago. What a terrible amount of trouble and expense in washing that sheet white, and after all

---

* This refers to a map, showing the proportion of negroes to whites in the different slave States, as indicated by darker or lighter shades.

I am afraid we shall only variegate it with blood and dirt."

After his month's visit to the capital, Hawthorne returned home much improved in health and spirits. The change of climate and scene, the relief from literary work, and the excitement of the war-spirit, effervescing all around him, seemed to have a beneficial effect upon him, and he went back to Concord with apparently renewed strength.

"CONCORD, April 13, 1862.

"DEAR BRIDGE,—Yours enclosing two photographs of Prof. Henry is received.

"I reached home safe and sound on Thursday after a very disagreeable journey.

"It was a pity I did not wait one day longer, so as to have shared in the joyful excitement about the Petersburg victory and the taking of Island No. 10.

"I found the family in good health, except that Una has a cold, and Rosebud is blossoming out with the mumps, which the other two children will probably take in due course.

"They all think me greatly improved by the journey and absence, and are grateful to Mrs. Bridge and yourself for your kind attentions.

"Your friend ever,
"NATH HAWTHORNE."

The letters just given show that though Hawthorne came to Washington "feeling not very
well," he returned greatly improved by the journey and the social life at the capital.

In that year and the one next following, he
published "Our Old Home," and did some other
literary work ; but the springs of life were running low, and the great brain was growing tired.

His lassitude increased, and he failed gradually till, on that last journey with Pierce towards
the White Mountains, the volume of his life was
closed.

The sad news reached me in Washington at a
time when I was confined to my room by an accident, and I could not join the little band of
devoted friends who mournfully bore his body to
its resting-place — upon the hill-top, and under
his favorite pines.

Pierce's regard for Hawthorne was warm and
tender to the last, and it became even more af·
fectionate as the end drew nigh.   The health of
Hawthorne had been gradually failing for two
or three years until May, 1864, when his brain-
power and physical strength both grew languid,
and he could work no more.   The ex-President
("Frank" of our college days) then came and
took him away towards the hill-country, with the
faint hope that the mountain air would reinvig-
orate him.

Travelling by easy stages in Pierce's private carriage, they passed through the region so familiar to Pierce until, on the 18th of May, 1864, they reached Plymouth, N. H., and stopped at the Pemigewasset House to rest and sleep.

On retiring that last, sad night, they occupied connecting rooms, with the door between them open. Hawthorne slept quietly at first, and Pierce went in two or three times to see to the invalid's comfort. The last time—about four o'clock—he found him lying in what seemed to be a quiet sleep; but the heart had ceased to beat. Hawthorne had died—apparently without a struggle.

The following letter of General Pierce gives an interesting and affecting account of Hawthorne's last journey and his death:

"ANDOVER, MASS., May 21, 1864.

"MY DEAR BRIDGE,—You will have seen, with profound sorrow, the announcement of the death of the dearest and most cherished among our early friends.

"You will wish to know something more of Hawthorne's last days than the articles in the newspapers furnish.

"He had been more or less infirm for more than a year. I had observed, particularly within the last three or four months, evidences of diminished strength whenever we met. The journey, which was terminated by Mr. Ticknor's sudden death at Philadelphia, was commenced at the urgent solicitation of friends, who thought change essential for him. Mr. Ticknor's death would have been a great loss and serious shock to H. at any time, but the effect was undoubtedly aggravated by the suddenness of the event and H.'s enfeebled condition.

"About three weeks since I went to Concord (Mass.), and made arrangements to take a journey to the lakes, and thence up the Pemigewasset with my carriage, leaving time and details of the trip to be settled by circumstances *en route*.

"I met H. at Boston, Wednesday (11th), came to this place by rail Thursday morning, and went to Concord, N. H., by evening train. The weather was unfavorable, and H. feeble; and we remained at C. until the following Monday. We then went slowly on our journey; stopping at Franklin, Laconia, and Centre Harbor, and reaching Plymouth Wednesday evening (18th). We talked of you, Tuesday, between Franklin and Laconia, when H. said—among other things —'We have, neither of us, met a more reliable friend.' The conviction was impressed upon me, the day we left Boston, that the seat of the disease from which H. was suffering was in the brain or spine, or both. H. walked with diffi-

12

culty, and the use of his hands was impaired. In fact, on the 17th I saw that he was becoming quite helpless, although he was able to ride, and, I thought, more comfortable in the carriage with gentle motion than anywhere else; for, whether in bed or up, he was very restless. I had decided, however, not to pursue our journey beyond Plymouth, which is a beautiful place, and thought, during our ride Wednesday, that I would the next day send for Mrs. Hawthorne and Una to join us there. Alas! there was no next day for our friend.

"We arrived at Plymouth about six o'clock. After taking a little tea and toast in his room, and sleeping for nearly an hour upon the sofa, he retired. A door opened from my room to his, and our beds were not more than five or six feet apart. I remained up an hour or two after he fell asleep. He was apparently less restless than the night before. The light was left burning in my room—the door open—and I could see him without moving from my bed. I went, however, between one and two o'clock to his bedside, and supposed him to be in a profound slumber. His eyes were closed, his position and face perfectly natural. His face was towards my bed. I awoke again between three and four o'clock, and was surprised—as he had generally been restless —to notice that his position was unchanged—

exactly the same that it was two hours before.
I went to his bedside, placed my hand upon
his forehead and temple, and found that he was
dead.   He evidently had passed from natural
sleep to that sleep from which there is no wak-
ing, without suffering, and without the slightest
movement.

"I came from Plymouth yesterday and met
Julian in Boston.   He said that his mother and
sisters were wonderfully sustained and composed.

"The funeral is to take place at Concord,
Monday, at one o'clock.   I wish you could be
there.   I go to Lowell this afternoon, and shall
drive across the country to C. to-morrow evening.
I need not tell you how lonely I am, and how
full of sorrow.

"Give my love to Mrs. Bridge.
                    "Your friend,
                         "FRANKLIN PIERCE.
"H. BRIDGE, ESQ., Washington, D. C."

Five years after Hawthorne's death Pierce himself died.

I trust that it will not be considered out of
place for me to give General Pierce's description
of his own ill-health, and his recollections of his
old friends and compeers, as in his last year he
realized that his end drew nigh.

In a letter, dated a year before his death, he wrote as follows:

"CONCORD, N. H., Oct. 11, 1868.

"MY DEAR BRIDGE, — It was refreshing to glance at your note of the 31st ult. But I can only acknowledge; I cannot reply to it.

"I do not spring up readily from my serious illness. My friends, who are around me, seem to think that I am regaining strength as fast as I ought to expect, at my period of life; while it seems to me that about all that can be said is that, within the last few days, I am holding my own.

"Oct. 15th.—I was obliged to drop this on the day of its date, and have not much strength now. When the physicians said I was convalescent, two weeks ago, I supposed I might be quite on my feet again by this time. Does it ever occur to you, Bridge, that we are rightly classed among the old men now? It is quite certain that those who were not old, but prominent, during my day, and those who were in the early struggle with me—among the first class Mr. Sullivan, Mr. Bartlett, Mr. Jos. Bell, Mr. Atherton, Sr., and Mr. Farley; and among the second Judge Gilchrist, Mr. Choate, Atherton, Jun., and at last Mr. Norris, Mr. Wells—and most of their more humble compeers, have gone before.

HAWTHORNE'S GRAVE

"I do not, my dear friend, look upon it gloomily, but sometimes, when I seem to be gathering up vigor so slowly, I doubt if I take into the account, fully enough, my protracted and severe illness, or the fact that nearly sixty-four years of pretty strenuous life have passed over my head. I am driving out, more or less, daily, and can repeat, with more or less comfort, 'Thou art my God, my time is in thy hand.'

"Give my love to dear Mrs. Bridge.

"Always, early and late, y'r Friend,

"FRANKLIN PIERCE."

A few weeks before his death Mrs. Bridge and I went to see General Pierce, who was then lying ill at his sea-shore cottage. He was too weak to leave his bed, and he was sadly emaciated; but his old, bright look came back as he welcomed us.

When we took our leave—all being conscious that it was for the last time—he raised himself from his pillow and embraced me like a brother.

And thus we parted.

CHAPTER XVI.

LETTERS OF MRS. SOPHIA A. HAWTHORNE.

UNQUESTIONABLY Nathaniel Hawthorne owed much of the success in his career to the cheerful aid and encouragement of his wife. She held up his hands when he was listless or despairing, she made his home a happy one, and she brought out the sunshine of his nature even when the clouds of life were darkest.

It goes without saying that Mrs. Hawthorne was a woman of high intellectual gifts. Capable of thoroughly appreciating her husband's rare qualities, and always ready and earnest to cheer and brighten his path, their union was most fortunate, and the world owes much to the wife's felicitous influence over her gifted husband for the results of his literary labors.

I have thought that, as a corollary to the foregoing sketches of Hawthorne, some of his wife's letters to me might fittingly be contributed, in order to show his manliness and loving devotion to his wife and family, as well as in displaying more fully some of his finer characteristics.

"CONCORD, July 4, 1845.

"MY DEAR SIR,—I wrote you a long letter some days since, which, not meeting entire approval from my lord, I laid aside. It was only a freak of fancy that was condemned, however, and so I will write the same letter over again, with that omission, for in all matters of taste and fitness he is absolutely correct. I must say to you again that I like your book very much for various reasons. Its truth and sincerity and unprejudiced observation make it valuable, independent of its excellent sense. It has the grace of simplicity and ease, and is, at the same time, sufficiently strong. It is also very entertaining. I am extremely fastidious in books, and am seldom held fast by one, but this I could not bear to lay down whenever I had a moment to read it. For your sake I am glad your cruise ended so soon; yet, for the sake of the public, I could wish it had been longer, that we might have had two volumes instead of one. There cannot be too much of such true and living history of countries and peoples.

"How impossible to find the limit to the consequences of a good action! Through your magnanimous desire to benefit my husband you have given the public a pleasant glimpse of Africa. Now my husband has returned your favor of the past with regard to his 'Twice-Told-Tales.' You first procured his appearance in a book, and now he introduces you in a fair volume to the present age.

"With regard to our visit to you, I fear you know not what you undertake. Unless I have a servant with me I cannot go, and a servant would make our party too large. I know that your hospitality is as magnificent as that of the Grecian hero who slew an hundred beeves to entertain his guests; but this is no reason why it should be abused. There would still be an advantage in my taking my woman, because she would take the whole care of us, and we should be no additional trouble to your domestics. But are not four of us too many? I wish, too, you would tell me about the military arrangement of your citadel. Is there a great deal of martial music and parade, so that Una's sleep would be murthered every noon? Her little life is rounded with a sleep every day, and if these naps are prevented, I will not answer for her serenity and agreeableness of behavior; and you might wish her in Jericho instead of in your house. I must be perfectly frank with you, dear sir, in another regard. The length of our visit to you will make a great difference about our household arrangements here, and therefore I wish you would not think me wholly wanting in etiquette and propriety if I request you to tell me whether you desire

us to stay one, two, or three weeks. I sincerely
wish to know which. I believe you appointed
the 25th of July for the appearance of our con-
stellation in your heavens. Is it not so? We
certainly could not appear before that time. Your
beautiful engraving of the Transfiguration shines
down upon us superbly all day long. I too should
like to command gold, so as to perform such splendid acts for my friends. I have often thought it
would be enchanting to be an Aladdin's Lamp,
and astonish people with unexpected pearls and
diamond houses.

" Una says she wishes very much to see Mr.
Bridge, and to go to Portsmouth and breathe
sea-air. When I question her upon the subject,
the enthusiasm of her assent far surpasses our
insignificant yes. In her eloquent speeches she
always points with the forefinger of her right
hand, which proves the legitimacy of that gesture
in oratory. Her language continues in that un-
intelligible, divine idiom to which we have no
grammar nor lexicon.

" My husband is spending this great day upon
the river. He has not yet said he shall go to
Portsmouth. He thinks he is too poor, I believe;
but I shall persuade him to the contrary, I suspect. Una wishes to be remembered to you,
with the gracious permission to kiss her lily-
white hand. I am very sorry I have had to write

with a spoiled steel pen, but perhaps you can make out my name. With cordial congratulations upon your new dignities, I am yours with much regard.

"S. A. HAWTHORNE."

"SALEM, Dec. 20, 1846.

"DEAR MR. BRIDGE, — My husband enjoins upon me to answer your very welcome letters of August 20th and October 20th, which he received yesterday. As he has a high regard for you and an utter detestation of pen, ink, and paper, I am glad to relieve him of assuring you, by means of these appliances, how cordially we remember you, and how rejoiced we always are to hear of your safety and well-being. I find my husband calls you 'the truest and warmest friend he has in the world.' From him such an assurance is, in my opinion, equal to a crown of glory. Besides most kindly thinking of you from an inward impulse as a friend in need and deed, we are perpetually reminded by the African idol upon the mantelpiece of Mr. Horatio Bridge.

"Una often inquires after you, and now understands perfectly that you are upon the great sea in a great ship. She is still a charming little person, though, like the moon, she holds her course sometimes behind clouds and slender storms, but they can only for a short time conceal her shin-

ing smiles and gracious countenance. I have
never discovered any ugliness in her heart and
behavior, for wrong has hardly power to cast a
shadow upon her before she breaks forth all con-
trition and sweetness. She is in perfect health
and bloom, and just now enchanted with the
snow, which, for the first time, she is big enough
to play with.

"Her little brother is an entire contrast to her
ladyship. His father called him the Black Prince
during the first weeks of his life, because he was
so dark in comparison with her. He is decidedly,
I think, a *brun ;* but his complexion is brilliant
and his eyes dark gray, with long black lashes,
like Mr. Hawthorne's. We thought he looked
very much like you at first, but he does not now.
He is a Titan in strength and size, and though
but six months old, is as large as some children
of two years. His father declares he does not
care anything about him because he is a boy, and
so I am obliged to love him twice as much as I
otherwise should. He is as pleasant and smiling
as a summer's day, and his temperament is very
sturdy and comfortable, quite unlike Una's, in
not being at all sensitive ; nor is he as delicately
organized. She enjoys him very much, and he
admires her beyond all things.

"We are residing in the most stately street in
Salem, but our house is much too small for our

necessities. My husband has no study, and his life is actually wasted this winter for want of one. He has not touched his desk since we came to Salem, nor will not, until we can remove to a more convenient dwelling, I fear.

"I am very glad to have such good news of your book. The old and new world seem to agree in its favor. It certainly has had a wonderful success, and I am quite content that you are writing more. I believe that you will write better than ever, now that you are a husband and a happy man, for marriage, with true sentiment and comprehension, is, I think, a great apocalypse, and opens a new world. I rejoice that you have ceased to be a stray comet, and have come into a regular orbit, for I should imagine you to be a person who might particularly enjoy a harmonious domestic life.

"I only saw Mrs. Bridge once, and then in the street in Boston, after your departure, for I found it impossible to call upon her before the birth of my little boy. She was with her mother, and I greeted her and shook hands with her very cordially. She looked very lovely in blue, but pale. I hope I shall know her some day, for her face and manner promise a noble and lovely woman. It seems to me that human beings are wretched Arabs until they find central points in other human beings around which all their brightest and

richest sentiments shall revolve.   Every true and
happy family is a solar system that outshines all
the solar systems in space and time.

"Mr. Hawthorne will write a postscript and tell
you about the war, of which I know nothing except the gratifying fact that Lieutenant ———
was shot.   Sincerely yours,

"S. A. HAWTHORNE."

"CONCORD, April 5, 1864.

"MY DEAR MR. BRIDGE,—Mr. Hawthorne has
gone upon a journey, and I opened your letter
this morning.   When you write anything I must
not see you must put *private* at the top of the
page, and then I will reverently fold up the letter
and put it aside.

"Alas! it was no 'author's excuse' which was
published in the *Atlantic*, but a most sad and serious truth.   Mr. Hawthorne has really been very
ill all winter, and not well, by any means, for a
much longer time ; not ill in bed, but miserable
on a lounge or sofa, and quite unable to write a
word, even a letter, and lately unable to read.   I
have felt the wildest anxiety about him, because
he is a person who has been immaculately well
all his life, and this illness has seemed to me an
awful dream which could not be true.   But he
has wasted away very much, and the suns in his
eyes are collapsed, and he has had no spirits, no

appetite, and very little sleep. Richard was not himself, and his absolute repugnance to see a physician, or to have any scientific investigation of his indisposition, has weighed me down like a millstone. I have felt such a terrible oppression in thinking that all was not doing for his relief that might be done, that sometimes I have scarcely been able to endure it—at moments hardly able to fetch my breath in apprehension of the possible danger. But, thank Heaven, Mr. Ticknor has taken him out of this groove of existence, and intends to keep him away until he is better. He has been in New York at the Astor House since last Tuesday night, a week from to-day. I have had six letters, five from Mr. Ticknor, and one at last from my husband, written with a very tremulous hand, but with a cheerful spirit.

"My dear Mr. Bridge, you, with your deep, warm, tender heart, can easily imagine how I have suffered in all this. My faith has been tried in its central life. I bless God it has not failed me ; but yet I cannot conceive of myself as surviving any peril to my husband. Though I would not complain, because I know that God must do right, and that he is also love itself.

" I should not be surprised if you should see Mr. Hawthorne in Washington. I wish he could be persuaded to stay southward until these piercing east winds of spring abate here. But he

intends to go a little later to the Isle of Shoals,
to stay until the advent of visitors in the fashionable season. I see that Concord is not the place
for him. He needs the damp sea-air for health,
comfort, and enjoyment. I wish, with all my
heart, that our dear little Wayside domain could
be sold advantageously for his sake, and that he
could wander on sea-beaches all the rest of his
days.

"The state of our country has, doubtless, excessively depressed him. His busy imagination
has woven all sorts of sad tissues. You know
his indomitable, untamable spirit of independence
and self-help. This makes the condition of an
invalid peculiarly irksome to him. He is not a
very manageable baby, because he has so long
been a self-reliant man ; but his innate sweetness
serves him here, as in all things, and he is very
patient and good.

"Julian has just entered upon his last half of
freshman year. He comes home every Saturday
and spends Sunday with us, so that we hardly
have lost him. He stoutly hates the Mathematics, but is very fond of Latin, and friendly to
Greek, and is the greatest gymnast in his class.
He is very strong and very gentle, and—you will
forgive a mother for saying this—he is entirely
of the æsthetic order, and his absence and unob-
servance of worldly considerations will probably

not advance him in the dusty arena of life; but
he will be unspoiled for the next world, I think,
and I hope he will be able to make at least a living in this.

"Rosebud is blooming out vastly. She is
nearly a head above Mama, and will be very tall.
She is now discoursing music on the piano, for
which she has a good faculty; and she goes to
school, and has a talent for drawing figures. Una
is very well, and feels excessively aged since her
twentieth birthday, though Julian assures her she
looks only sixteen. She has no tutor now, but
studies by herself in the morning, and paints in
the afternoon, and sews for the soldiers a great
deal. I have written you too much, dear Mr.
Bridge; but you ask me after all these folk, and
so I tell you. With my kindest regards to Mrs.
Bridge, I am   Very truly yours,

"S. A. HAWTHORNE."

"THE WAYSIDE, CONCORD, MASS., Nov. 7, 1865.

"MY DEAR MR. BRIDGE,—Can you send me
any memories or incidents of Mr. Hawthorne's
college life, when you were with him so much?

"I am now very much occupied in copying his
journals, or portions of them, for papers for the
Atlantic; and something is demanded of his life,
and these records in his own words are the best
of all autobiography—I mean are the best biog-

raphy, being *auto*. They are very rich as studies of nature and man, and now and then a glimpse of his personal character gleams through in a radiant way, though he puts himself aside as much as possible, as always. The Augusta *Journal* is all copied, in which I have ventured to put Mr. B. for your name. You figure there in a commanding way, being lord of the Manor in position and character.

"The reason I wish to have you write down your reminiscences is because, by and by, these papers will all be collected into a volume, and these connecting links will be wanted. The earliest remaining journal begins in 1835.

"I have requested his sister to write her recollections of his childhood and early youth, for she alone can now do that.

"It is a vast pleasure to pore over his books in this way. I seem to be with him in all his walks and observations. Such faithful, loving notes of all he saw never were put on paper before. Nothing human is considered by him too mean to ponder over. No bird, nor leaf, nor tint of earth or sky is left unnoticed. He is a crystal medium of all the sounds and shows of things, and he reverently lets everything be as it is, and never intermeddles, nor embellishes, nor detracts. It is truth itself, and has all the immortal charm of truth, even in the smallest details. For do we not like to see even a common object of still life truthfully represented by the great masters of Dutchland? It is only the great masters in any art who trust to truth.

"I hoped to see you again, summer before the last, with Mrs. Bridge. My constant expectation of seeing her prevented me from replying to her very kind letter. Will you tell her so with my love? Perhaps she will come this next summer, if she can bear to come now my king has gone, and so the cottage is no longer a palace.

"I shall be glad of any occasion to hear from you, dear Mr. Bridge.

"Very sincerely yours,

"SOPHIA A. HAWTHORNE."

"CONCORD, MASS., Nov. 25, 1865.

"MY DEAR MR. BRIDGE,—I have both your letters, for which I am deeply obliged. I feel great compunction in asking you to take your time to recollect the past in regard to my husband, for it seems as if you ought to rest when you leave the Bureau. But I beg you not to weary yourself in doing it, for there is no pressing hurry, though, as you truly say, 'we should do without delay what is to be done.' I mean that this is not to be done if it tax you too much.

"Gen'l Pierce has indeed been alarmingly ill,

but is now recovering. Julian happened to come home to forage for books, and I sent him to Concord, N. H., immediately, to see exactly how he was. Julian found Gen'l Pierce very weak, and unable to sit up, and fearfully wasted, but not 'blue,' as Julian expressed it, and very glad to see him, and Julian read aloud to him. It was a bilious affection that prostrated him. The day after Julian's return, Thursday, 23d, he was well enough to think of sending me a newspaper containing a paragraph about his improvement in health.

"As 'gratitude is the keen sense of favors to come,' according to the witty Frenchman, I wish to know whether you can help me to any autographs of persons notorious and illustrious in the war times. I have a dear friend in England (dear to Mr. Hawthorne, too), who is always writing eloquent implorings for autographs of great Americans—great in treason, great in patriotism, great in council, great in prowess. This English friend has done so much for me, in sending me the finest picture in the world of my husband, that I would beg for him anything that is respectable. If you cannot attain to these autographs, and will tell me to whom I might properly apply, I will take any trouble whatever for the end in view.

"Your last letter is very interesting to me.

Mr. Hawthorne always scorned the idea that he had ever written any poetry. And I never saw any he wrote except a single poem which is in his own handwriting, given to me, I believe, by his sister. But I never dared let him know I possessed it, for he would have forbidden me to keep it, probably. His ideal was so high, and his modesty so excessive, that he was never satisfied with anything he accomplished, even to the last. But his first efforts he utterly despised.

"I hope you will recall characteristics of his early youth. Do you remember the scene with the gypsy in Brunswick? Of a woman who told fortunes?

"I hope you are very well, dear Mr. Bridge. Those friends of my husband's whom he loved so faithfully are very precious to me. There were but few—you and Gen'l Pierce the chief. But I feel a vital interest in your and in his health and well-being. I hope you are better than when I saw you here.

"With our love to you and Mrs. Bridge,
    "Very sincerely yours,
        "S. A. HAWTHORNE."

    "January 19, 1866.

"MY DEAR MR. BRIDGE, —To-day I received your kind note and the paper of reminiscences, for which I thank you exceedingly. Once be-

fore (Nov. 24) I received a paper from you, which
I acknowledged at once, and at the same time
asked you if you could procure me some autographs of our famous men of the war, statesmen
and generals, for an English friend, to whom
my husband had promised some. It is a matter of great moment with this gentleman, and
every time I have a letter from him he mentions
his hopes and expectations. I cannot bear to
trouble you, but I do not know to whom else
to apply; and I feel bound to fulfil Mr. Hawthorne's intentions, especially in regard to Mr.
Bright, who loved him so truly.

" I have a very lame right hand, and so I cannot write but a few words, or I should enlarge
upon these very interesting particulars about Mr.
Hawthorne.

"Gratefully and cordially yours,
"SOPHIA A. HAWTHORNE."

" 1866.

"MY DEAR MR. BRIDGE,—To-day I received
your letters enclosing the autographs. I cannot
express how much obliged I am to you for them,
for Mr. Bright writes from time to time a pathetic
appeal for the fulfilment of the promise made
him. He has lately met with a severe bereave-
ment in the death of a brother, who was the pride
and hope of the family, and it is the first time in

a large circle that one has been taken; but I
shall send him the autographs.

    *   *   *   *   *   *

"You must excuse me for not thinking Mr.
Hawthorne over-valued you. I never heard from
him but one opinion on this subject. He had the
utmost reliance upon you, and reposed upon it
with infinite satisfaction. It seems to me not a
small merit to have inspired in him such respect,
love, and trust as he invariably expressed for you.
That you do not recognize yourself in his portrait
only makes it the truer. I always felt that he
had no more thorough friend than you in the
world, and I know he thought so.

"How very kind of you to find me these autographs. I thank you over and over for them.
We all send our love to you and Mrs. Bridge.

"Very cordially yours,
          "S. A. HAWTHORNE.

"P.S.—For your last reminiscences I am deeply obliged. Every word you record is to me like
apples of gold in pictures of silver, because I can
so absolutely trust your truth and sincerity. You
see I am smitten with my husband's great prejudice in your favor.—S. H."

              "Jan. 2d, 1867.
"MY DEAR MR. BRIDGE,—I take the liberty to

enclose this letter to you, because I do not know whether General Hitchcock be in Washington or not, and I did not wish my letter to go to the Dead-letter Office. He used to live on Pennsylvania Avenue. If you will put the address on for me I shall thank you very much.

"I send to you and Mrs. Bridge all Christmas and New Year good wishes. I have been confined to my room for three weeks, but am now better. The children are all well and satisfactory. Rose has just left me, having been at home through the Christmas holidays. She is now at Dr. Lewis's famous gymnastic school in Lexington. Julian is reading his logic and metaphysics. Una reads history to me and the literature suggested as she goes on. She also is keeping up her music and Latin, and has a class in gymnastics. They are all so bright and good that my life is a thanksgiving for them. I live for them. When they are settled in life I should like to sleep as *he* did, if God please. Affairs perplex and tire me very much, yet I am in great peace.

"I hope you and Mrs. Bridge are well. I fear you are too busy to tell me how you do. With my love to Mrs. Bridge, I am,

"Very sincerely yours,

"SOPHIA A. HAWTHORNE."

In conclusion let me hope that, while gleaning a few grains in the field of Hawthorne's history, I shall have contributed something which will, at least, have the value of personal testimony, and which may, perhaps, be used with advantage by some biographer in the future.

I may also hope that the disclosures herein made will give a modicum of pleasure, unalloyed by adverse criticism, to those who are near and dear to me.

To them I commend this little volume.

THE END

JAMES'S HAWTHORNE.

Nathaniel Hawthorne. By HENRY JAMES, Jr.
12mo, Cloth, 75 cents. ("English Men of Letters Series.")

Mr. James's estimate of Hawthorne's novels is singularly
calm, judicious, and correct. He is not eulogistic, but he is
altogether appreciative, and there has nowhere been given a
better, if so good, a study of the inner nature of Hawthorne's
works.—*Philadelphia Times.*

The fine insight into the subtle mysteries of human character, with the rare power of presenting its most elusive traits
in significant language, which has given a peculiar charm to
Mr. James's novels, has been called into vigorous exercise in
this masterly estimate of the great American writer of fiction.
—*N. Y. Tribune.*

This biography has charming qualities. Its grace, clever-
ness, artistic proportions, its half tones, its modulated tints,
its general air of the best literary society, make it a very
agreeable companion.—*Christian Union, N. Y.*

Mr. James has made an important contribution to the
literature of criticism in America.... He has made a careful,
conscientious, and even vivid literary portrait, such as few
of our own writers could have made, we may say with safety.
....It may indeed be said to be saturated with the essence
of literary criticism, and to be a fine thing in itself.... It is
penetrated by its purpose, and, in a very graceful and charming way, its total effect is made to leave upon the reader the
consistent and single impression with which it is clear the
author sets out, and which he nowhere loses sight of.—
Nation, N. Y.

PUBLISHED BY HARPER & BROTHERS, NEW YORK.

☞ *For sale by all booksellers, or will be sent by mail, postage prepaid, to any part of the United States, Canada, or Mexico, on receipt
of price.*

BOSWELL'S JOHNSON.

Boswell's Life of Johnson, including Boswell's Journal of a Tour to the Hebrides, and Johnson's Diary of a Journey into North Wales. Edited by GEORGE BIRKBECK HILL, D.C.L., Pembroke College, Oxford. *Edition de Luxe.* In Six Volumes. Large 8vo, Leather, with Cloth Sides, Uncut Edges and Gilt Tops, with many Portraits, Views, Fac-similes, etc., $30 00.

Popular Edition. Six volumes. Cloth, Uncut Edges and Gilt Tops, $10 00.

This great work has now reached a form which may be considered definitive and final....Is in every way the best edition ever published.—*N. Y. Mail and Express.*

Dr. Birkbeck Hill's edition of Boswell may perhaps be regarded as the most scholarly, painstaking, liberal-minded, fair, and complete that has yet been published. It is honest work throughout, and careful and loving work, and it is informed by a sanity and ripeness of judgment, and illustrated by an extent of information which must place and keep it in the front rank.—*N. Y. Tribune.*

The student of the period, and the reader who has loved his Boswell with a life-long love, will thoroughly enjoy the intellectual treat provided for them by the editor of this beautiful edition.—*Spectator*, London.

Altogether this edition is one to warm the cockles of the heart of both bibliphile and literature-lover.—*Hartford Courant.*

That this edition is the best goes without saying, and that it is a monument of labor will astonish no one who reflects that eighteen years have been required to produce it. A more competent editor than Mr. Hill cannot be imagined.—*Literary World*, London.

PUBLISHED BY HARPER & BROTHERS, NEW YORK.

☞ *For sale by all booksellers, or will be sent by mail, postage prepaid, to any part of the United States, Canada, or Mexico, on receipt of price.*

The Journal of Sir Walter Scott, 1825–1832, from the Original Manuscript at Abbotsford. With Two Portraits and Engraved Title-pages. Two Volumes. 8vo, Cloth, Uncut Edges and Gilt Tops, $7 50.
Popular Edition. One Vol. 8vo, Cloth, $2 50.

Full of interesting glimpses into the great author's mind, and reveals in a striking manner the inextinguishable buoyancy with which he encountered misfortune, the iron perseverance with which he set himself to clear away the mountain of debt with which he found himself burdened when his best years had passed, the keen sense of honor and duty which marked even his most private communings with himself, and the gay humor which characterized him whenever the clouds parted for a moment and permitted the sunshine to pass. . . . It is indeed a valuable contribution to our knowledge of Sir Walter Scott.—*N. Y. Tribune.*

A piece of transparent simplicity, free from moralizing and free from attitudes, in which Scott shows his heart and writes down his thoughts, experiences, and personal records.—*Independent, N. Y.*

Mr. Douglas is a conscientious and competent editor, and he has supplied all the notes which are required for elucidating the text without making a parade of superfluous learning. . . . This final work by Sir Walter Scott is as instructive and welcome as any which he penned.—*Athenæum, London.*

A better tempered, less morbid diary never was published. . . . No extracts can do justice to the book as a whole—to the manly, cheerful, tender spirit of the man.—*N. Y. Herald.*

This is such a book as the world has not often seen. These two impressive volumes contain one of the most effective pictures of a really strong man, painted as only that man himself could have painted it, which the English language contains. . . . This book is one of the greatest gifts which our English literature has ever received.—*Spectator, London.*

Published by HARPER & BROTHERS, New York.

☞ *For sale by all booksellers, or will be sent by mail, postage prepaid, to any part of the United States, Canada, or Mexico, on receipt of price.*

MOTLEY'S CORRESPONDENCE.

The Correspondence of John Lothrop Motley, D.C.L., Author of "The Rise of the Dutch Republic," "History of the United Netherlands," "The Life and Death of John of Barneveld," etc. Edited by GEORGE WILLIAM CURTIS. With Portrait on Steel. Two volumes. Royal 8vo, Cloth, Uncut Edges and Gilt Tops, $7 00; Sheep, $8 00; Half Calf, $11 50.

The charm of these letters lies in the personality of the writer, which makes itself felt throughout; in the finish and vivacity of his literary style; and in the inherent interest and wide variety of the subjects that came up for familiar treatment in the course of his many years' residence abroad.— *Critic*, N. Y.

A worthy memorial of the historian and diplomat, and an honorable addition to our national biographical literature.— *Boston Transcript.*

Mr. Motley's correspondence is a boon to book-lovers, and is well worth purchasing, as it is beyond all question well worth reading. In a word, this correspondence may be truly said to be a most valuable addition to a most pleasant department of literature, and as such it deserves all the success which we most confidently anticipate for it.—*Spectator*, London.

A more entertaining collection of letters has not been published in the century. Their author was a man of rare culture, of keen observation, and of polished wit.—*Observer*, N. Y.

The most delightful book of an autobiographical character that has been published in this country for many years.— *N. Y. Sun.*

An honor to literature, and to American literature especially. They give us the more intimate history of a man of genius, a great writer, and a man of the world—*N. Y. Tribune.*

PUBLISHED BY HARPER & BROTHERS, NEW YORK.

☞ *For sale by all booksellers, or will be sent by mail, postage prepaid, to any part of the United States, Canada, or Mexico, on receipt of price.*